Quiet Magic

Also by Pauline McKinnon

In Stillness Conquer Fear, Collins Dove, Melbourne, 1983; Newleaf/Gill & Macmillan, Dublin, 1999

Rainbow's End, Collins Dove , Melbourne, 1987

Footprints in the Sand, Collins Dove, Melbourne, 1988

Joseph's Secret, Collins Dove, Melbourne, 1989

Help Yourself and Your Child to Happiness, David Lovell Publishing, Melbourne, 1991

audio CDs

Stillness for Stress-Free Living, Pauline McKinnon Life Development, 1999

Let's Be Still, Pauline McKinnon Life Development, 2002

Quiet Magic

A Parable about finding happiness

PAULINE McKINNON

David Lovell Publishing
Melbourne Australia

First published in 1990
this revised edition in 2002 by
David Lovell Publishing
PO Box 822
Ringwood Victoria 3134
Australia
Tel +61 3 9879 1433
Fax +61 3 9879 1348

Cover design by Donna Rawlins
Typeset in 12.5/15.5 Adobe Garamond
Printed and bound in Australia

National Library of Australia
Cataloguing-in-Publication data

McKinnon, Pauline.
Quiet magic : a parable about finding happiness.

For children aged 7-12 years.
ISBN 1 86355 090 9.

1. Relaxation - Juvenile fiction. 2. Meditation for
children - Juvenile fiction. 3. Stress in children -
Prevention - Juvenile fiction I. Title.

A823.3

For Tom, Margie and Jim Taylor
and because of
Lachlan, Kate,
Susannah and Stephen

Contents

Chapter 1

Jimmy Candlestick was in a bad mood. It was Saturday morning and he was all alone. His mother and father were out at work and Jimmy had no-one to talk to and nothing to do. Even worse, he had a sore throat.

With his mouth wide open Jimmy stood in front of the mirror and peered at his reflection, searching for his tonsils. His throat was red and dry. Swallowing hurt. He frowned hard at himself and poked out his tongue because he didn't like what he saw.

The mirror showed a young boy with a mop of fair bouncy hair. The blue eyes were kind and the small, straight nose might have been well suited to a sprinkling of freckles. But the kind eyes were also sad, and there were no freckles because Jimmy was hardly ever in the sunshine. Most of his time was spent within four walls, operating the computer or watching television.

Jimmy ran the hot tap and spent a few minutes trying to flatten the bounces in his hair with hot water. But even *that* wouldn't go the way he wanted it to.

He then decided to play around on his computer, but he couldn't access anything that interested him and then the system crashed completely. Jimmy stamped and screamed and even kicked the wretched thing in frustration.

'Just my luck,' he yelled. 'Just when I wanted to try that new program, too.'

Jimmy threw himself down in front of the television.

'Rotten sport,' he moaned. 'Nothing but sport, sport, sport.'

Jimmy hated sport because sport wasn't a part of his life. Jimmy had never even been for a jog through the local park — and he certainly had never kicked his own footy or held a cricket bat.

He tried the radio.

'Boring,' he said out loud.

Then he remembered music ... but the electronic organ was boring, too. He knew by heart every tune he could play on it.

The shelves in the TV room were crammed full of video movies but Jimmy had already seen just about every movie there was to see. He looked gloomily at his mobile phone, but who would he call? He considered his huge electronic game collection, but nothing there excited him either.

'Nothing to do, no-one to talk to. Stupid day. Stupid Saturday. Stupid, boring, horrible day. I *nearly* wish it was a school day,' Jimmy said to himself, feeling more and more edgy and grumpy by the second.

But for Jimmy, even school days were boring. Going to school meant going from his own room to a special room upstairs, where he learnt everything from a robot. The Candlestick family owned a team of robots that did all the work. And so that he would learn perfectly, this included teaching Jimmy what other children learn when they go off to normal school. So, apart from robots and his busy parents, Jimmy had never even made a friend.

Jimmy Candlestick lived with his mum and dad on the top floor of a luxurious building in the middle of a busy, polluted city. Of course many people live a bit like that but they usually go outside and enjoy the rest of the world. Apart from family outings in a fast car, the Candlestick family spent almost all their lives indoors. The result of this was that Jimmy rarely saw the sunshine, or felt the rain, and had never even jumped into a puddle!

He had no cat, no dog, not even a canary, for the robots and his mother didn't like birdseed on the carpet. And the only flowers Jimmy had ever seen were the floral arrangements that his father sent to his mother when she was cross.

Jimmy didn't know what trees were like, nor did he know the songs of wild birds, for the windows of the building were double glazed — to protect the air conditioning system.

Jimmy had been missing out on a great many things. But he didn't know that he was missing anything because his parents provided everything anyone could possibly want — right there at home. In fact, they only left home to go and earn more money to buy more things — though there really wasn't much room left to put anything else anyway. The family walked on carpets as soft as kitten's fur and they owned enough treasures and knick-knacks to sink a battleship. Every gadget you could possibly imagine was theirs. And they also owned their own private gym and amazing entertainment centre at home so that the family could amuse themselves without having to go outside at all.

At night the robots served the family dinner. Unfortunately, robots are not great cooks, and they do tend to drop precious plates. So the family usually ate pre-packed frozen dinners, ready to serve, from throw-away dishes. This meant that their diet consisted mainly of potato chips and icecream. No wonder Jimmy's face was so pale!

There was a great deal of noise in the household, too. This was a jangly bangly constant noise, like a symphony orchestra with every musician playing out of tune.

The robots rattled and groaned. The electronics beeped. The televisions blared constantly and loud hisses, squawks and bangs came from all the many machines in this very mechanical place. The Candlestick home was very busy, noisy, rushed and fast — as if, always, an emergency was about to happen.

When darkness fell, Jimmy and his mother and father went to sleep with their fingers still twiddling from all the buttons and knobs that kept the place going. And despite all the noise, they'd hardly spoken a word to each other throughout the day — because this family wasn't very good at talking and laughing together at all. So, for Jimmy, home was a very lonely place from dawn to dark.

On this gloomy Saturday morning Jimmy was surely the

most miserable and grumpy boy in the world. Not only did he have a sore throat but his head had begun to ache as well. His personal robot registered this fact and relayed it to Jimmy's mother via the mobile phone she always carried in her handbag.

'This is very unusual,' Mrs Candlestick murmured as she checked the screen. She had the very latest equipment of course, and she could see that Jimmy was looking forlorn and unwell. 'I must send for the doctor', she said.

She entered the computer code for 'doctor' on her transmitter and continued rushing about the busy city.

When the doctor arrived at the Candlestick's place later in the morning Jimmy was staring dejectedly at the blank TV screen. He had flicked and twiddled every switch in the house, and now it seemed there was nothing left but to let the hours drag by.

The doctor was a short roly-poly man with hardly a hair on his head and the twinkliest blue eyes you have ever seen. His round face was covered with lots of crinkles and lines, which were made from the happy smiles he gave to lots of people.

Not surprisingly, his name was Dr Smiley. He took Jimmy's temperature and gave him a dose of pink medicine. Then he gave Jimmy a pat on the shoulder and one of his big smiles, telling him he would soon be well again. As Dr Smiley did this, Jimmy began to cry. Big wet tears rolled down his cheeks to the floor, making quite a damp patch on the furry carpet.

'Whatever is the matter?' asked Dr Smiley. 'You're not *that* sick, you know.'

Jimmy cried even more. At this moment he was no longer surly and miserable; he felt really, really helpless and sad.

'Come on, Jimmy,' said the doctor. 'Things aren't so bad … let's have a smile.'

Jimmy, who didn't know why he was so upset, gurgled between his tears that he felt sick … and bored … and mixed-up … and he had no-one to listen to all his troubles, except for the robots, who were of no use in that way, and, worse still, here was Dr Smiley wanting him to smile and be cheerful…and Jimmy was more sad and lonely because of this…because he didn't know how to *smile* at all!

The doctor looked very shocked at hearing all this. He was so shocked that his eyes nearly popped out of his head.

'Do you mean to tell me that you can't *smile*? Why, smiling is the most important part of feeling better again — whether you have the measles or seasickness, or you're just plain scared. What am I going to do with you?' And Dr Smiley flung himself into the nearest chair to consider the problem.

A moment or two ticked by and then the doctor spoke. 'Tell me Jimmy, have you got a grandmother?'

Jimmy shook his head.

'No grandmother,' mused the doctor. He thought a little longer. 'An ageing aunt, perhaps?'

Again Jimmy shook his head.

'No grandmother, no aunt,' muttered the doctor. His mind was working busily.

'A next-door neighbour then?' The doctor looked hopeful, but Jimmy, standing there sadly, shook his head again.

Dr Smiley was puzzled. Then he had an idea.

'I'll lend you mine!'

'Your what?' said Jimmy.

'My grandmother, of course,' the doctor answered briskly. 'Grandmothers are wonderful for helping people to smile. Yes, yes, yes. You must visit my grandmother. I am prescribing it.'

And without further ado, Dr Smiley picked up the telephone and asked to speak to Jimmy's mother and father.

When he had finished the conversation he said to Jimmy, 'Excellent … excellent. Your parents have taken my advice and are sending you to my grandmother's house immediately. You'll like her, I'm sure. Her name is Mrs Fender because she's strong and protective. And *she'll* be able to help you find your smile — I guarantee it!'

Jimmy had hardly any time to think about what was going on before his parents arrived home. They set the robots to work, packing some things and, with a quick good-bye, they bundled Jimmy into a taxi. Almost before he knew what was happening, Jimmy found himself the only passenger in an aeroplane on his way to his destination.

Chapter 2

On the plane Jimmy's throat was hurting and his head was aching. He became restless and bored again so he plugged in the headphones and closed his eyes to listen to some music. Shortly, the music stopped and Jimmy opened his eyes to find that the plane had landed in a very different place. This place may not have seemed unusual to most people, but it certainly did to Jimmy. The sky was not grey or stained with smog, but clear and blue. There were no tall buildings but wide, fresh, open spaces dotted with cows and sheep, happily munching the grass. Rolling green hills were divided by white fences. Tall trees surrounded pretty buildings quite different from those where Jimmy lived. Jimmy didn't know where he was, but he guessed he had been flown to the country. He had seen places like this on television.

Hesitantly climbing out of the plane (which immediately soared into the sky again), Jimmy saw only one path to follow, a narrow, winding track. With clenched hands and a heavy heart, he started along it, to meet the doctor's grandmother, Mrs Fender.

Now, Jimmy was a boy of very few words. As he trudged along, clutching his bag, it occurred to him that he was all by himself in an unknown place, on his way to meet an unknown grandmother, and without even a robot to tell him what to do to or what to say. Jimmy began to worry. When people worry, they forget to think pleasant thoughts and they don't see and feel and hear all the exciting and interesting things around them.

So Jimmy was worrying about being in this new place, and whether he would have to stay for a long time, whether he'd like the food, and whether he'd be able to watch his favourite TV programs. He was worrying about why his parents had sent him here, and whether he should have even come. His sore throat and headache worried him, and he also worried about not being able to smile. And because he was worrying so much, he didn't even notice the beauty and peacefulness all around him.

The track had wound its way across the slopes and beyond the cows until it crossed a bridge over a stream. And now it meandered invitingly through a forest.

This forest was filled with the softness of the morning dew, the freshness of a new-born breeze and the gentleness of a shadow. Through the branches above, pockets of morning sunshine filtered to the earth, warming all that lived there. Moist ferns nodded, sheltering younger ferns spangled with spider webs. If Jimmy had been listening he would have heard the rustle of the wings of busy birds. If Jimmy had been watching he would have noticed wildflowers — splashes of colour here and there as if spilled from an artist's palette to decorate the earth. If Jimmy had been more relaxed he would have run into the leaves, tossing and crunching them underfoot and smelling the scents of the forest. But all Jimmy could do was worry.

Soon the track met a quiet country road, and by the side of the road stood a house. Brightly painted white with a red roof and a white fence all around the secluded garden, this was one of those cosy houses that come straight out of picture books, even to the cat on the mat and the last pink hollyhock.

With a start, Jimmy realised that he had arrived. He felt a little scared but he had come here to learn how to smile and get well again, so he moved towards the gate. There was no noise. There were no cars, no aeroplanes and none of the sounds that surrounded the busy city. This quietness caused a new worry, and Jimmy was just about to run back the way he had come when he heard someone calling his name. There before him was Dr Smiley's grandmother.

'Hello,' she called. 'You must be Jimmy. The boy who wants to learn how to smile. I've heard all about you. Come in, come in!' And she held the gate open wide and waved him through with a flourish.

Jimmy had expected someone quite different from this lady. He had pictured a frail little old woman wearing a smiling face and a black shawl, for he had seen such grandmothers on television. Instead, he saw before him a graceful lady with an easy step who wore bright and cheerful clothes that were not very different from the clothes his mother wore. True, she was old. She had lots of lines on her face, like Dr Smiley, and a knot of snowy hair that was escaping into tendrils about her cheeks. However, she didn't look frail but calm and strong — just as Dr Smiley had mentioned — and she had the twinkliest eyes Jimmy had ever seen (even twinklier than Dr Smiley's).

11

'Hello,' whispered Jimmy, stuttering a bit and wondering whether a sound would come out.

'Mmm, yes, a few smiles would be an improvement,' Mrs Fender murmured, surveying him at arm's length. 'How's that sore throat? ... And I believe your head's aching too?'

'Still sore,' Jimmy replied gloomily.

'Ahh ... a good dollop of sunshine and a gulp of fresh air should help for a start,' Mrs Fender said, extending her hand warmly. 'You're very welcome ... come in. Your room is ready for you.' And walking ahead, she showed him into her house.

The room prepared for Jimmy was neat and simply decorated in blue, with soft curtains criss-crossing the window. From the window was a view of the sea. Jimmy, however, was busy searching for the television set, and there was none to be seen.

His fingers were longing to operate switches and his eardrums were tiring of the quiet.

Clutching his bag close to him Jimmy sat on the edge of the bed and said as politely as he could, 'Where is the TV set, please?'

Mrs Fender shook her head, 'No TV set, Jimmy.'

Jimmy's mouth fell open. What would he do without it? Well ... there must be a computer somewhere — everyone has a computer!

'Where's the computer then, please?' Mrs Fender shook her head again. 'No computer either, Jimmy.'

'What about some electronic games? A playstation maybe?' Jimmy was feeling desperate as his tense fingers twitched more and more.

Mrs Fender sat down beside him and spoke slowly.

'My dear Jimmy, this house has no gadgets at all. I don't disapprove of them really, but I just don't need them. You see, you've come here to learn to smile and be happy, and to do that you have to get to know *yourself*. We can never get to know ourselves if we are always being ordered about by machinery. Oh, they're very clever machines, I know, and I admire the people who invent them. And machines can be most useful, too, but no machine can ever match the workings of a real person.'

The workings of a person! What on earth was she talking about, silly old woman. Jimmy was really indignant. He slammed his bag down on the floor frowning with a sullen look in his eyes that showed how mad he was feeling.

Without a word Mrs Fender left the room.

Jimmy's prospects were not looking good. What a dumb place to be sent to. He wondered why his parents had agreed to let him come here.

'They don't care about me,' Jimmy concluded to himself. And he lay down on the bed, thumped the pillows a bit and then cried himself to sleep.

Time went by and Jimmy awoke a little later to a tap on the door. Lunch was ready. For a moment he forgot where he was. His eyes were sore from crying and he rubbed them, bringing back his memory. The frown settled again on his aching forehead and he sighed in disappointment. But the thought of food was tempting, so Jimmy rolled off the bed and slouched out of the room, following Mrs Fender to the kitchen.

Chapter 3

At the table Jimmy was served a bowl of steaming soup and a fresh brown roll. At least he was hungry and, as he ate, Mrs Fender peeled and quartered an apple. Jimmy watched her all the time and wondered why her robot was not doing this job. Aware of his eyes upon her, Mrs Fender tossed the quarters into a pretty glass dish and handed it to Jimmy.

'Well, Jimmy Candlestick, what are you thinking about?'

Jimmy hesitated and said sulkily, 'I thought you'd be smiling all the time.'

'Good heavens, who do you think I am — the Cheshire cat?', she laughed softly, 'True smiles are not something you wear like a pair of gumboots! Smiles come from being happy. They come from inside and happen all by themselves.'

Jimmy looked a little crestfallen. And with that she did smile, and all the crinkles on her face fell into place, her eyes sparkled and she put out her hand across the table and patted Jimmy's. Just for a moment, Jimmy almost didn't mind being there at all.

'Come, Jimmy, let's make a start on this lost smile of yours. You may not see here all the gadgets that you have grown up with, but I think you will soon discover that there are other ways to find a smile. I can help you begin your search if you'll let me. Will you come with me on this adventure?'

Jimmy didn't want to do anything with anyone but, having nothing else to do, he agreed.

Together they left the table and went down the passage. Mrs Fender opened a door to a bright room overlooking the garden. The room was bare apart from a couple of chairs, a table laden with brushes and paints, and an easel. The walls of the room were lined with portraits of boys and girls whose faces smiled out at Jimmy. Clearly they were happy, so what was she going to show him?

On the wall at the end of the room was a mirror. Mrs Fender drew Jimmy towards it.

'Tell me what you see, Jimmy.'

Jimmy turned away. He had seen himself this morning in the mirror at home and had hated what he saw. In this mirror, the reflection would be no different. There was nothing to smile about here. Just because all those other goodie-goodies in frames were looking pleased, why should he try? He hated his own appearance anyway. He shifted his weight from one foot to the other and dropped his shoulders, his expression becoming more sullen.

'It's only a mirror, Jimmy,' Mrs Fender said gently.

'I don't want to,' scowled Jimmy, and again he sighed deeply and folded his arms across his chest.

'Don't you like looking in mirrors?'

'Nuh,' said Jimmy staring at nothing in particular on the floor. He wished she'd leave him alone.

Mrs Fender sat down at the table. She selected a brush and began dabbling with some paint.

'Have you forgotten why you came here, Jimmy?' she murmured.

'Nuh'.

'Didn't you want to come?'

'Not really,' sighed Jimmy, turning his eyes to the ceiling.

'You came here, but you didn't want to come?' Mrs Fender said. She was using her brush at the easel now and had pushed her glasses down to the end of her nose for better vision.

'Well, I had to, didn't I,' stated Jimmy.

'Mmm. Maybe. But then usually if people don't want to do something, they say so. Did you do that, Jimmy?'

'Nuh'.

'Mmm,' said Mrs Fender.

Jimmy looked at her. She had paused holding the paint brush aloft, and was gazing questioningly at Jimmy over the top of her glasses. Her lips were pursed in mid-sentence and she seemed faintly amused.

There was silence.

Jimmy fidgeted uncomfortably.

Mrs Fender put down her brush and straightened up, regarding Jimmy warmly.

Jimmy was sorry he'd been impolite. She was kind to him. He wanted to tell her what he was feeling, but he didn't know how to. His tongue, not much used to speaking, felt completely tied.

But he had no need to try. Mrs Fender broke the silence.

'Come and tell me what you think of this,' she said, beckoning Jimmy to the easel.

He was glad to go.

There in front of him was a portrait of himself. Well, it must have been him. The figure in paint had *his* hair and *his* nose and was wearing *his* tee shirt. But the face was blank. There were no eyes and there was no mouth.

Jimmy felt relieved because he didn't really have to see himself after all.

'Who is this?' Mrs Fender asked.

'Well … I s'pose it's me … me, without a face,' Jimmy said.

'Without any *expression* on your face,' nodded Mrs Fender. 'You didn't want to see the sad face. That's why you wouldn't look in the mirror. Am I right?'

Jimmy nodded.

'Well, now you have a choice. You may have whatever expression you wish painted into this portrait. How would you like to see yourself?'

'Happy,' said Jimmy.

'All…right.' Mrs Fender picked up a pencil.

'We'll put a smile here — like this.'

And she drew in a large smile that was a bit like a clown's smile.

Jimmy was pleased.

'That's better,' he said.

'And you look happier in reality now, too,' said Mrs Fender. 'So, we'll give you some eyes — because eyes hold the smile that's within, you know.' She drew in two large round eyes.

Jimmy brightened. Mrs Fender was rather clever. The face was really like a clown now. Jimmy's head with a clown's face. It looked funny and Jimmy began to laugh out loud.

'Is that the way you want to see yourself, like a clown?' Mrs Fender seemed surprised.

'No...oo,' giggled Jimmy. 'It's not really me...'

'Exactly,' said Mrs Fender. 'It's not you at all.'

'I just want to look, you know, good,' said Jimmy, searching for words.

'And *that's* why you came here,' said Mrs Fender, 'to look and to feel *good*?'

Jimmy nodded again, this time enthusiastically.

'Excellent,' said Mrs Fender, rubbing out the clown's face.

'We'll leave this unfinished portrait here on the easel. When you find your smile, you *will* be looking and feeling good — and I'll be able to paint the real Jimmy's face. Now let's get started. It's a lovely sunny day. We'll go out to the verandah.'

Jimmy felt uncertain.

'How are we going to do it?' he asked. 'I mean, well, you made me laugh just then — seeing myself as a clown. That's OK isn't it? What else do we have to do?'

Mrs Fender took Jimmy's hand, leading him out of the room.

'*Laughing* — or giggling — is easy, Jimmy. Anyone can laugh like that. People laugh at funny films. They laugh at jokes, they laugh at the weather, they laugh even if they trip over. Mean people sometimes laugh at other people. And some people even pretend to laugh whether they're feeling happy or not. So laughter doesn't always tell a true story.

But, a smile … now that's different. Smiles come from within and tell a different story. People who truly smile are relaxed and happy. They've discovered a lot about themselves and they've learned to live more freely — and so their inner smile comes more freely. Then when they laugh, their laughter is free and natural and happy too. So, in answer to your question Jimmy, to find your true smile what we have to do is help you discover the *real* Jimmy Candlestick!'

Jimmy felt very strange … kind of mixed-up and wanting to cry, but ashamed to. He wanted to speak, too, but, again, he didn't know what to say. Mrs Fender was really asking him to change — to be different somehow. He knew that, and he wanted to, but then, he didn't want to either. It was safe being the way he was. Deciding to change is a bit like trying to walk, blindfolded along a slippery path. There *might* be someone there to catch you if you fall, and it *might* be wonderful when you arrive at the other end and take off the blindfold, but until you do it you don't know! Yet Jimmy didn't want to stay the way he was — lonely, sick, miserable and without a smile. So he had a decision to make.

There was a long silence between them as Jimmy considered Mrs Fender's words.

Then he looked at her. Her kind eyes returned his gaze and she smiled again. Suddenly Jimmy felt very much like climbing onto Mrs Fender's knee and curling up there forever. At that very moment Jimmy was extremely grateful to Dr Smiley for the loan of his grandmother.

Chapter 4

Jimmy felt reassured when he looked into Mrs Fender's twinkly eyes. If she had promised him adventure, then adventure he would have. Suddenly Jimmy realised that he trusted Mrs Fender, which was a new feeling. When you live mostly with robots you don't have to trust much at all. It felt good to trust. So Jimmy sat down on the verandah with her, on a shiny white chair with a bright red cushion that matched the roof of the house, and waited.

Of course, it was very difficult for someone like Jimmy to wait. He had never had to wait for anything in his whole life. He was used to dashing from one piece of technology to the next, pressing keys and adjusting dials and getting instant results. At home he finished his school work at the touch of a button, and when he was hungry he dialled a meal. He could spend hours on e-mail communicating with strangers thousands of kilometres away — and when he tired of all that he could click the mouse and do something else. Just about everything Jimmy had ever known until today had happened immediately.

Now this waiting was *terrible*. Jimmy's fingers twitched like mad, his toes jiggled and his eyes darted here and there on the lookout for *anything*. Then Jimmy began to fidget and bounce up and down on the red cushion because sitting still was so dull, and his eardrums throbbed, longing for noise. He crinkled up his forehead and squeezed his eyelids together and frowned and bounced a bit more and wished that something would happen.

Because nothing was happening Jimmy thought he would practise smiling. He tried hard to stretch his lips into what he thought a smile should be like, and his face began to ache. Then he opened his mouth right up, wide as a gateway, and tried and tried to laugh. Very slowly he said, 'Ha! Ha! Ha!', trying to think of something funny but nothing like a smile appeared. A small beetle saw Jimmy's open mouth and flew in for a quick look around. Its wings tickled Jimmy's throat and he began to cough and splutter, so the beetle hastily flew away. And all the coughing made Jimmy's sore throat hurt again.

Mrs Fender, who had been quietly observing Jimmy, began to speak. Her voice was soft and kind and so soothing in the silence that Jimmy remembered again his trust in her and didn't feel quite so bouncy.

'Do you remember, Jimmy, when I told you earlier that in order to learn to smile and find happiness you need to know yourself?' Jimmy nodded.

'And you understand that I've lived a long time and have seen lots and lots of people, both happy and unhappy?'

'I suppose so, ' said Jimmy, looking closely at all her lines and crinkles.

'Well,' continued Mrs Fender, 'all the happy people know themselves very well and all the *unhappy* people *become* happy by *learning* to know themselves more. They do this by being quiet sometimes — by being still — and by using less effort to achieve wonderful things in their lives.'

'What sort of things?' interrupted Jimmy, sitting on his hands.

Mrs Fender thought for a moment and then said, 'Adventures, really, but I can't tell you exactly which adventures because everyone's adventures are different and special to themselves. But I *can* tell you that if you learn to be still and quiet for a while each day, as I show you, you too will have adventures — better than you've ever dreamed of.'

'I don't understand.' Jimmy looked puzzled.

'Of course you don't — not yet anyway. But believe me, there's no need to understand. Just trust me. There's a kind of magic here if you want it.'

Magic! Now that *was* bewildering! Whatever did she mean? This really added to Jimmy's confusion.

But as she spoke Mrs Fender's face crinkled up again in a gentle smile, and her expression was so kind that even though he was still puzzled he said with a sigh of acceptance, 'What do you want me to do?'

'I don't want you to do anything. Just be still. Rest your feet flat on the floor and your hands in your lap.'

Mrs Fender paused.

'Now … just let your eyes close. Good. That's good. Let your eyes gently fall closed and feel the stillness of your whole self. There's no need to do anything, or make any effort at all. Soon you'll notice that all your muscles relax… and after a while you'll sense the silence all around you. There's no need to think about anything either. Just enjoy the silence. Just enjoy being *still.*'

23

Once more Jimmy had his doubts. He did as she asked, but he hated being still. He hated closing his eyes in this new situation in case he might miss something, and he felt uncomfortable sitting upright like that. He was trying hard to please. His breath felt tight and his head ached even more.

'This isn't going to work,' he said aloud. 'I can't just sit here. You can't find things by doing nothing. Anyway, I thought you were going to help me. I can't do this by myself. I've never been still and quiet before, ever. I don't know how to. If being still and quiet is going to find my smile then why can't you do that for me while I start looking?'

Mrs Fender shook her head but her eyes were smiling.

'What would be the use of me doing it for you?' she asked. 'It's *your* smile, not mine, that's missing. When we're trying to find ourselves, only we ourselves can do what we have to do to achieve that. Now, Jimmy,' Mrs Fender spoke rather firmly, 'learning to be still and quiet and *very relaxed* is the most important step in your search for your smile. Without this, nothing will be discovered at all. I can teach you what to do, but only you can do it for yourself. And the best way to succeed at this is by not *trying* to make anything happen at all. Shall we begin?'

Jimmy thought Mrs Fender was talking in riddles. But clearly there was no way he could escape this lesson, so he closed his eyes again and hoped for the best.

The sun was warm and Mrs Fender's voice was very soothing as she spoke softly about being calm and natural, effortless and still, and Jimmy was soon surprised to realise that sitting in the sun with your eyes closed was rather pleasant. However, he couldn't sit *still*. He wanted to hop up and run off to find something else to do. So he jiggled and twisted and felt uncomfortable and wished that Mrs Fender hadn't shown this to him after all. But she was still murmuring peaceful words and as she spoke she gently rested a calm, cool hand on Jimmy's forehead, washing away his restlessness with a soothing presence.

Remarkably, little by little, Jimmy stopped jiggling and twisting. After a bit longer, almost without him knowing, Jimmy was sitting upright in a very relaxed way, not doing anything at all. Suddenly it felt easy doing nothing. Mrs Fender had stopped speaking and now everything was quiet. Presently, as he sat there, Jimmy began to feel *really* good. Nothing much was on his mind and now that his fingers had stopped twiddling and he was not bouncing or trying to smile or frown or do anything at all, Jimmy quite liked the stillness — and the warmth of the afternoon sun.

The silence that had at first been boring now seemed to protect him. It was beautiful being still. Jimmy had never known anything like it before. It was so beautiful that there was no need to even bother to think. All those things that usually buzzed around in his head seemed to be resting, too. All Jimmy knew was that he was there and that he was doing nothing and that this kind of nothing was the best thing he had ever done. And then a very special question popped into Jimmy's head: could this be something like the kind of magic Mrs Fender had promised?

After a time Mrs Fender spoke softly again, and slowly

Jimmy opened his eyes, blinking a little at the beautiful world. He breathed deeply, feeling refreshed, and for the first time ever, the scent of newly mown grass and the distant call of a bird came to him. These were new experiences, indeed.

Mrs Fender rose from her chair beside him.

'How's that sore throat?' she asked brightly, with a hand on Jimmy's shoulder.

'Not so bad,' murmured Jimmy, dreamily. 'And my headache is gone, and I'm not tired any more!' He felt pleased. He surveyed the whole view from the verandah, taking in the freshness of it all.

'I…think I might go for a walk. May I?'

This was about the best sentence Jimmy Candlestick had ever spoken in his whole life and Mrs Fender was delighted.

'Go,' she cried. 'Explore and see what you can find, but don't be late for dinner at six o'clock'. And she waved him away and disappeared into the house.

Chapter 5

Jimmy went out the gate. He started down the road towards the sea. He walked faster and faster until he was running. He reached the top of a slope of creamy sand and jumped into it. Jimmy could feel his heart beating loudly and the blood streaming through his body and it felt great. He rolled over and over and down and down in the sand until finally he stopped at the edge of the water. And he sat there watching the waves, as the tide crept closer, wondering why he had never felt so good before. Jimmy had a feeling that he was beginning to understand something that Mrs Fender wanted him to know.

As he sat there looking around him his eyes fell upon a stream trickling towards the water's edge. This was the stream that he had crossed earlier in the day and here it met the sea. Jimmy thought this would be the perfect place to begin exploring, as Mrs Fender had suggested, so he set off towards it.

Summer had dried the mouth of the stream, leaving rocks embedded in the sand. Jimmy used the rocks as stepping stones and made his way into shallow water towards the shade of the forest.

He had not gone very far when he heard a voice calling.

Jimmy stopped and looked around but there was no-one to be seen.

Then he heard the voice again, coming from a clump of waterweed nearby. Jimmy peered into the weed to find a fat, feathered duck. She was as white as snow, with a yellow bill and bright black eyes.

'Where *have* you been?' quacked the duck. 'I've been waiting and waiting, and I thought I'd have to spend another cold night out here!'

Jimmy's surprise at hearing a duck speak to him faded when he saw that the duck was trapped. She had been caught around the foot by a piece of string which was tangled among the weeds.

'You poor thing,' said Jimmy fishing in his pocket for his nail clippers. 'How long have you been stuck here?'

'A couple of days,' replied the duck. 'I called out to you earlier when you crossed the bridge but you ignored me.'

'Oh no,' said Jimmy. 'I didn't mean to ignore you—I'm so sorry. I didn't hear you. I had a sore throat and a headache and I was scared because I was going somewhere new and I wasn't thinking and … oh, I *am* sorry …'

'Never mind, never mind all that,' quacked the duck impatiently. 'Just hurry up and get me out of here, please. My foot has gone to sleep.'

And she tried to demonstrate what she meant by balancing on one large, yellow webbed foot and immediately falling over with a small splash into a little pool beside her.

Jimmy got to work with his clippers and soon had her untangled.

'Thank you. Thank you, indeed. I am most grateful.

Now may I introduce myself?' And, with that, the fluffy white duck shook her dainty head and fluffed herself up even more. For a moment she stood stall and erect, and then, because her foot was still asleep, she promptly tumbled over again.

Jimmy thought she was beautiful and felt very concerned that she was distressed by her ordeal. He had never touched a real bird. Now he longed to pick this lovely creature up, to save her from falling all the time.

'Do you live here in the forest?' he asked.

'Yes, yes, I *live* here. But I'm not a native,' she added hastily. 'I'm just an inhabitant, nesting upstream.'

Then she tossed her head, indicating the forest, and said, 'That's where the natives live. Hundreds of them. Birds, possums, lizards, snakes — the lot. We all get along very well together and they don't mind me here among them. Sometimes I long for a few kitchen scraps, you know, but on the whole this is a good place to be.

'Would you let me carry you to your home?'

'Very well,' conceded the duck, a little subdued since her introductions had not quite gone the way she had intended. 'Mind you don't squash me. It's not far,' she added with a look of contentment, and, closing her eyes, appeared to fall asleep.

Jimmy picked her up gently. To his surprise her feathers felt smooth like satin, only much stronger and filled with life, and he could feel her heart beating and little ripples of movement as she rearranged her wings.

Jimmy carried her carefully, hoping he would be able to find where she lived. He need not have worried, for soon the bundle of feathers in his arms stirred and a pair of bright eyes flew open. The duck raised her head, gave a couple of gentle quacks and then spoke.

'My nest is just nearby. See, there among those lilies. If you put me down I shall sleep until morning, when my leg will be quite recovered.'

'Won't you need food?' questioned Jimmy, noticing a bed of neatly hollowed grasses. He placed her in it.

'No, no. Not yet. In the morning I shall breakfast on snails.' She paused, quacked loudly and then, tilting her head to the side in the prettiest manner, said to Jimmy, 'Thank you so much for rescuing me. I'm most grateful. You *are* a nice boy. In fact, I think you're quite a gentleman.'

Jimmy had never received a compliment like this before (especially from a duck) and he felt so flattered that he didn't know how to reply. Then he remembered something that had been puzzling him.

'How do you know how to speak to me? Is it magic?'

'Ah,' said the duck, 'I was wondering when you'd ask me that. The answer is very simple. All creatures know how to speak to one another, but many of them don't bother listening to each other most of the time. Maybe it's magic … I don't really know.'

This answer satisfied Jimmy's curiosity and seemed perfectly reasonable, but there was one more question.

'My name is Jimmy. What's your name?'

'Miranda,' said the duck graciously. 'I was given that name by a young lady about your age who came here once. It's much better than Quack-Quack or Cuddles, don't you think? And now I'd like to rest. You may visit again

30

tomorrow, my friend. Off you go before it gets dark.' And she fluffed her feathers, nestled down among the lilies and fell asleep.

Jimmy watched her for a few minutes until he saw that the shadows had lengthened and all that was now visible of Miranda was the glowing whiteness of her feathers in the twilight. The sun had gone down and the forest had become quiet, ready for sleep, but Jimmy could only think of what Miranda had called him — 'my friend.'

'I've got a friend,' said Jimmy aloud. 'A friend, a friend, a friend! Oh, what a day!' And he jumped up, splashed across the stream and climbed up the mossy bank on the other side. Again and again the words rang in his ears and he ran back towards Mrs Fender's house. Then he remembered where he was running to, and that Mrs Fender had told him not to be late for dinner. And he realised that he had not only one friend but two — all in one day. Two special friends that *he*, Jimmy Candlestick, was important to. He ran faster until he reached the white house, jumped over the gate, and bounded up the path and through the door.

'I've found a friend, Mrs Fender. I've found another friend,' he cried with shining eyes.

Mrs Fender smiled, nodded wisely and said nothing. Instead she continued serving dinner on a *real* china plate.

The two sat down together to a delicious piping-hot meal straight from the oven and, as he swallowed, Jimmy's sore throat hardly hurt at all. Excitedly, Jimmy told Mrs Fender about all that had happened during the afternoon, and she listened to everything he said.

Soon after dinner Jimmy went to bed. He didn't even

ask about watching TV or playing computer games. He slept soundly and restfully, lulled by the roll of the sea. Instead of dreaming about numbers on a screen or robots bringing him breakfast or fast cars on a highway, Jimmy dreamed of creamy feathers and castles in the sand. And when he awoke it was a new day.

Chapter 6

The first thing Jimmy Candlestick noticed was that his sore throat had gone. Then, as he blinked his eyes open, he remembered the soft white duck who had become his friend. He reached out, searching for his computer to get a reading on her condition. But, of course, there *was* no computer here! Jimmy realised that if he cared about Miranda he would have to go to her and see her for himself.

He jumped out of bed and ran towards the window hoping that she might be close by. He had never really looked out of a window before. In fact, he realised all of a sudden that he had been looking at things all his life and had never really seen *anything* until now.

Wide and blue, beckoning and beautiful, the sea stretched before him, glittering with sparkles that danced upon it like a million fragments from a giant mirror. The sun was still rising hot, sending out shafts of warmth, and the whole morning seemed to smile. Jimmy wished he could keep the moment forever.

Jimmy recalled Miranda's words about creatures speaking to one another but not listening most of the time. He thought about this while taking in the view before him and said to himself, 'I bet lots of people don't bother to *look* either.'

Throwing on his clothes he ran out the door to find his other friend, Mrs Fender, to tell her about this new discovery. As well as finding new friends and seeing the world around him, Jimmy was beginning to discover more and more words also. This was a big change from his usual reliance upon a keypad!

Mrs Fender didn't seem to be around the house, and Jimmy was looking forward to breakfast.

He had never prepared a meal before, especially not breakfast. His robots had always handed it to him ready to eat, and now Jimmy was faced with the choice of going without or using his initiative. His hunger decided for him. He searched the cupboards and the refrigerator. There was orange juice and milk. Nearby on the table stood a jumbo loaf of crusty bread and a basket full of red shiny apples, still bearing their leaves and sprinkled with dew.

Jimmy's mouth watered at the thought of those crisp juicy pieces of apple. If Mrs Fender could slice an apple surely he could do so too.

He found a knife, which was rather too large for the job, and began to peel the apple. This was more difficult than he had imagined. His fingers were only used to pushing and twiddling, not holding, bending, peeling or slicing. The sharp knife missed the apple and sliced cleanly into Jimmy's finger, shedding blood all over the floor. Jimmy yelled. He yelled so loudly that Mrs Fender appeared from the garden to see what all the fuss was about. She saw Jimmy frozen to the spot, clutching his hand and making a lot of noise as tears began to roll down his cheeks. In a flash, but very quietly, Mrs Fender had Jimmy's hand under cold water and was soon gently drying it with a towel. Part of the towel was becoming pink from the bleeding finger and Jimmy was trembling and sobbing and very red in the face. Mrs Fender carefully inspected the cut, while Jimmy shook even more.

'It's not serious, Jimmy. You were very lucky. Fingers bleed a great deal if they're cut, and that makes the injury look worse than it is.' Her voice was calm and kind. Jimmy turned his head away, as he couldn't bear to look.

'It's not *really* hurting is it?' said Mrs Fender.

Jimmy screwed up his face, cried a bit more and said, 'Yes,' very loudly.

'Oh, come on,' said Mrs Fender. 'You're making it much worse than it really is. Now I have to use some special disinfectant, and then I'll bandage it for you.'

Jimmy shuddered and held the towel closer over the cut. Mrs Fender sat him on a chair and left him for a moment, returning soon with the dressings. She started attending to his injury.

'Jimmy, screwing your face up like that *makes* things hurt you know. And holding your hand so tightly with the other one also makes it hurt. And why are your legs twisted all around the legs of the chair?'

'To stop me from shaking,' Jimmy managed.

'I think you'll find,' said Mrs Fender in a very gentle voice, 'that you'd stop shaking a lot faster if you let go a little. And if you don't loosen your hand, how can I bandage your finger? And that tightened up face is making it all feel worse. Now please, Jimmy, just let yourself become easy. Let go like you did when I showed you how to relax on the verandah yesterday. Remember? Let your arms loosen and your legs go floppy and feel your face relax, and I'll fix your finger.' For a moment she placed her cool hand on Jimmy's forehead and then she gently prised his hands apart, holding the injured one firmly and letting the other drop into Jimmy's lap. Then just as gently, Mrs Fender untangled Jimmy's legs from the chair. And Jimmy stopped shaking! His tears stopped flowing and he looked down at his finger calmly, surprised to see that it wasn't such a bad cut after all.

Mrs Fender cleaned and bandaged the wound and then she looked at Jimmy.

'Now what was all that fuss about?'

Jimmy looked rather embarrassed. 'I don't know. I've never cut myself before. I've never even used a knife, but I wanted to try. I thought my finger was hurting but it isn't at all. Why isn't it hurting, Mrs Fender?'

Mrs Fender laughed softly. 'Jimmy,' she said, 'most unpleasant things that happen don't hurt as much as we think they might. When we become tense and frightened, all these things hurt more.'

'But once I bumped my elbow on a brick wall and it hurt. The robot told me to clench my teeth and bear the pain.'

Mrs Fender looked a bit cross. 'Just as I might have expected,' she said. 'Many people act like those robots of yours, too. They teach others to tighten up and fight pain. But that's not how it works. Have you ever watched an animal in pain?'

36

'No. Oh, well, Miranda … yesterday. Oh help! I was on my way to visit her when this happened. I hope she's all right. I must go now.'

'I'm sure she is quite all right,' said Mrs Fender, handing Jimmy some buttered bread. 'Finish your breakfast and then you can go. But before you do, won't you sit quietly for a while, just as you and I did yesterday? It makes your day much easier, and remember it's all a part of finding your lost smile, too.'

Jimmy was impatient to get away but he agreed. Mrs Fender had been so kind.

'I guess there might be something good about sitting still, in a way, but I don't know why there should be,' he said doubtfully, as he ate. But then he thought of the fun he had had yesterday, and the little adventure of meeting a talking duck, and the sunlit sea and the forest, and learning something about friendship.

He spoke again, 'Miranda was a bit cross because she'd been trapped there for ages with no-one to help her. But she wasn't wriggly or crying or anything, like me. I suppose *she* knows how to sit still?'

'Very likely,' agreed Mrs Fender. 'Birds and animals rely very much upon nature to help them. They only need extra help from us when they're injured beyond their control, either by disease or, as Miranda was, by some type of trap. But usually they just wait patiently and help themselves. So, you see, sitting still is part of nature and humans can use it, too.'

'All right. I'll sit still for a little while now and then I'll go to Miranda,' Jimmy said. He got up from the chair to help Mrs Fender clear the table, quite unaware that never before had he done anything like this. Strangely, he was not missing the robots around the house very much any more.

When Mrs Fender returned to the garden Jimmy put a whole apple into his pocket and went out the front door of the house to the verandah.

He wondered what he'd be doing at home, 'I'd be in my room at my computer, or watching television or perhaps taking lessons from a robot. That's sitting still, isn't it? But then using a computer means using fingers and thoughts and eyes and ears and even legs, twisted around chairs! Even watching TV uses a lot of effort and concentration, and as for school work with the robots, well, I jiggle all the time'.

Jimmy dragged a chair to a warm sheltered corner, and sat down to close his eyes and simply *be*, just as Mrs Fender had shown him yesterday.

At first he wished he hadn't done this because he was fidgety again.

'What a waste of time,' he thought. 'I wanted to get started on adventure. Now I'll be late. The day's half over. Miranda might have gone away … what if I can't find her again.' His thoughts tumbled on and on, with all kinds of ideas flying through his mind.

But the sun was warm and as Jimmy let himself relax a little, he didn't feel in so much of a hurry after all. And then there was that wonderful easiness again, as though nothing was difficult to do any more. Every single muscle loosened all over his body, from his toes to even higher than his eyebrows. As his body relaxed more and more, all discomforts disappeared and once again Jimmy felt wonderfully still. Soon his thoughts also became quiet and still, so that he didn't even have to think. All he had to do was enjoy that special feeling of tranquil peace.

Jimmy was able to stay like that for a while and when he slowly opened his eyes he wasn't restless or twitchy — he felt really *happy* and strong, and quite grown up.

Breathing easily, he practically had wings on his heels as he ran to the stream to find Miranda. She was there, where Jimmy had left her, pecking at weeds and ferns. He was delighted to see her but now he wondered whether he had only imagined their conversation yesterday. He approached her softly and sat down on the bank, fascinated by her movement— pecking here, preening there, shaking her fluffy tail feathers from time to time.

Suddenly Miranda turned and saw Jimmy. She froze, and then resumed her elegance, stretching her delicate head towards him as she spoke. 'For a moment I didn't know who was there, creeping up on me like that.'

'Sorry,' said Jimmy, who was very relieved that the little duck really did speak.

Miranda went back to her breakfast and then paused to say, 'I'm afraid I haven't time to chat right now. I have to eat quickly and then hide myself.'

Jimmy looked mystified.

'What do you mean?' he asked.

'The firedogs are back,' said Miranda between billfuls. 'Surely you know?'

'Well, no, I don't,' said Jimmy. 'Who are the firedogs?'

Miranda stopped pecking and looked anxiously about

her. Then she waddled towards Jimmy and nestled down beside him, concealed by the ferns on the bank of the stream.

'I'll tell you,' she whispered, 'but if you see strange creatures about, don't reveal that I'm here — I don't *think* they'll bother you, because you're human. I don't think the firedogs are interested in humans. Of course, you can never be sure...'

Jimmy felt alarmed. His eyes grew wide as he listened and he felt a prickly sensation down his spine.

A great lump came into his throat. Jimmy tried to speak to Miranda but no words would come so he decided to think for a minute instead. He thought about the firedogs. What did she mean? He was scared, but he could see nothing unusual, just the quiver of leaves, a few birds fluttering and the invisible breeze blowing the grasses on the bank. There was stillness all about him and Jimmy remembered the peaceful feeling of sitting quietly. Now he was glad that he'd done that.

Calmly Jimmy swallowed, finding his voice.

'Miranda,' he said gently, 'you scared me then. What on earth are you talking about? There's no danger here.'

'Well, we'll see about that,' she murmured. 'I'll tell you the story of the firedogs right from the very beginning, and then you can judge for yourself.' Jimmy snuggled closer to his new friend.

Chapter 7

'Hundreds of years ago,' began Miranda, 'from an unknown and distant planet called Uptight, somewhere up there in the galaxy, a group of its inhabitants came down here to Earth. They came to explore, and I expect they wanted some company, but soon they just began to help themselves to whatever they could. They like Earth, and so they keep coming back to camp here in the forest. These creatures are known as firedogs and they're very strange and scary animals. They look rather like the dogs that we know, but they are much larger. Instead of a coat of soft hair, they have a big shaggy coat and a mane like a lion. They walk on two legs and on top of their heads are two antennae,' Miranda paused, looking around, 'because they're *space* dogs!'

'Go on,' Jimmy urged.

'They don't bark, they speak like humans, and they're extremely grumpy. They steal and plunder and destroy, and, worst of all, they love animals and birds like myself — not to be friends with, but to roast in their ovens, which they light with a puff of fiery breath. That's why they're called firedogs. So you see why I'm afraid.'

'Yes,' Jimmy said. 'I certainly do! But can't someone send them away? I mean, surely if they're being a nuisance

41

and not behaving themselves, someone should send them straight back to where they came from.'

'It's not that easy', said Miranda. 'Firstly, they're pretty powerful and I doubt whether anyone on Earth could control them. But secondly, no-one — no human that is — knows about them, only we birds and animals of the forest.'

Jimmy looked amazed. He was beginning to follow her story.

'You mean these firedogs have been roaming around here, misbehaving for years and years and no-one has noticed?'

Miranda nodded. 'They like this forest because their spaceship lands in the sea nearby. They have no need for people, only things. So they live, undisturbed and hidden here in the forest, and they do exactly as they please.'

Jimmy thought for a while.

'Hasn't *any*one ever seen them? Surely someone must have come across them and asked them their names?'

'I shouldn't think so,' replied Miranda. 'Remember I told you yesterday that creatures don't bother to listen much to each other? Well, even if people *had* come across the firedogs, I doubt whether they would have bothered to listen to them properly. People are the only ones able to help, because they can *change* things. But then people only visit this forest now and then, so they don't see what is happening. We birds and animals can't change things. We just have to accept everything as it is.'

'I'd never thought of it like that,' observed Jimmy. 'The lives of all you creatures are almost completely in the hands of us humans.'

'Oh yes,' agreed Miranda. 'We get shot at and stood upon and chased with brooms, and fished for, and sprayed with poisons, and all manner of miseries. But some of us survive, because enough people are good to us. People like yourself, Jimmy, who care.' Miranda added in sudden inspiration, 'If more people cared about animals and birds and insects, they might begin to care more about each other, and then they'd be a lot happier.'

Jimmy was touched by Miranda's openness. Something was beginning to tell him just why that smile of his was missing. For years and years he'd been stuck doing the same things, acting in the same old ways, and never looking outside his own four walls. There was so much happening out in the world! It certainly was time to change. Jimmy made a decision.

'Miranda, I'm going to help you. I came here to find my smile and learn to be happy. I think I can see now where to begin. Mrs Fender has shown me how to be still and relaxed. That was a big step, for if I hadn't learned that I never would have even found the forest, or you, Miranda.'

The friendly duck quacked shyly.

'Now I want to learn more about myself and about others. Maybe this is what Mrs Fender means about having adventures. The next thing to do is to find those ferocious firedogs. Someone has to stop them!'

Miranda, her own fears subsiding, became so excited that she jumped up from the ferns and rushes and stood high with her wings outstretched, flapping them wildly in generous applause and quacking loudly to Jimmy her newfound hero.

'You can do it, Jimmy, you can do it!' she cried, and Jimmy felt very important indeed.

At that moment, however, just *how* he was going to do it, Jimmy did not know. But he had made a promise and he would keep it. He jumped up from the bank of the stream and paused.

'Miranda, I'm going to leave you now but please stay hidden and don't quack or make a noise, whatever happens. Of all the forest creatures I want to help, you're the most important, so take care.'

'Very well,' said Miranda. 'Thank you, Jimmy. I'll be waiting for you to return. Good luck!' And she disappeared into the ferns.

Jimmy had no idea where to look for the firedogs so he retraced his steps until he was back on the track above.

Away from the shade the air was hot and the once-gentle breeze became a fierce wind. Billows of grey cloud swallowed the blue sky, and the air felt heavy. A storm was brewing.

Pondering, Jimmy found his way back to the beach.

When Jimmy had tumbled onto it yesterday, and this morning when he had seen the ocean from his window, the sand was firm and golden, the water brilliant and blue. Now the beach was muddied and scattered with litter. Cans and bottles, papers and packets were everywhere. Some of the rubbish was printed with a kind of writing Jimmy had never seen before. It looked back-to-front and was certainly not like the writing he learned from the robots. Among the wreckage was the remains of a feast and nearby, still smoking, were the embers of a great fire. Jimmy shuddered. He knew he must be on the right trail.

As Jimmy stood on the shore wondering what to do next, he saw from behind the headland a large shape slowly rise from the depths of the sea. As he watched, the distant shape became a huge silver ship, settling in the shallow waters. This was no ordinary ship but a ship shaped like a football with round shiny windows. The ship had two spiky antennae and two tall legs, and it seemed to walk to the water's edge.

Jimmy crouched behind a clump of bushes and waited to see what would happen. As he did so, the first splash of rain hit the sand. A fork of lightning pierced the heavy sky and a moment later thunder clapped all around him. The wind, suddenly stronger, squashed the bushes and bowed the trees, whipping up the sand so that it stung Jimmy's legs.

Squillions of raindrops pelted from above, plastering Jimmy's clothes to his body. Soon the rain changed to hail, which covered everything like snow. Jimmy crawled deeper into the scrub, craning forward to keep his eyes on the silver ship, afraid he might miss something of importance.

He had never been in a storm. He had glanced at storms as he rushed past his window at home, but he hadn't heard the noise, smelled the air or felt the rain and wind of a storm. He was scared. For all Jimmy knew, he might be flattened by the thunder, struck by the lightning, drowned by the rain or washed away by the roaring sea. For a moment he wished he were safely back at Mrs Fender's house, not out here on some stupid mission to help a duck!

But thinking of Mrs Fender reminded Jimmy of

something very important — the way to relax. Here was a good chance to try it. He remembered not to squeeze up his mouth and eyes. He remembered not to tighten his arms and legs. He remembered to let go and not fight what he was feeling, and soon he became calm. He stayed quietly hidden, low in the scrub, watching the silver ship and feeling the living storm. It was not scary at all. Nature was at work, reviving the world and Jimmy felt the excitement of it all.

Then he saw them.

One by one, a small group of dark shapes appeared near the mouth of the stream, and walked towards the ship. One by one they boarded, shaking the rain from huge shaggy manes. The door closed and the spaceship rose on its legs and waded out to sea.

Within minutes it had lowered itself into the raging waters and disappeared behind the headland once more. The firedogs were gone.

But Jimmy knew they would be back. He was sure that it was the storm that had lured them to their ship in order to seek refuge.

'If they're scared off by a storm,' Jimmy said to himself, feeling very brave, 'they can't be too ferocious.'

He decided he must find the firedogs' camp in the forest once the storm was over. Perhaps then he would learn some more about them.

After a time the wind and rain grew quieter, and the lightning ceased. Jimmy didn't want to delay in case the firedogs soon returned, so he crawled out of the scrub and ran towards the stream. Glancing back he saw no sign of the ship, so he ran on in the direction from which the firedogs had come and out of sight of the shore.

Chapter 8

When Jimmy reached the bridge that crossed the stream he took shelter under it. He was hungry and the apple was still in his pocket. He sat down, polished his apple and began to munch. Its sweet juiciness helped him to collect his thoughts and he tried to form a plan.

Water, Jimmy decided, was the key to his success. No fire likes water. Water must be the firedogs' enemy, too. If he could somehow surround their camp with water, then he would be in a position of power, a position to reason or bargain with the firedogs so that they would no longer threaten the forest creatures. But how to do it? He must dig, or find a massive hose, or dozens of buckets. It seemed a big task for a boy but Jimmy was the only one to do it and he knew he didn't have a moment to lose. Finishing his apple he set off once more, his eyes searching for signs of the firedogs' camp. Further and further Jimmy went into the forest, splashing along the stream until he came to a clearing.

Here the trees were thinner and their rich foliage was blackened, their trunks scarred. In other parts of the forest thick grasses and ferns flourished, but here black and dank emptiness stretched ahead. There were no animals rustling, no birds singing. There was only the smell of fire.

Trees had been hacked and felled. There was strange writing on the bark. Rubbish lay about, too. Everywhere Jimmy looked he saw destruction, and in the middle of it all was a building, a shack made of dead branches. It was most certainly the camp of the ferocious firedogs.

'Ugh,' Jimmy said to himself. 'How could they?' Everything was spoiled.

If the firedogs were not stopped, there would soon be no forest at all. There would be no gentle animals or birds, either. The scene before him was like the end of the world.

Jimmy decided he needed help, and fast. This was not a job for one boy after all. He must get back to Mrs Fender's house and find others. However, Jimmy was curious and instead of dashing away as fast as he could, he scrambled up from the stream to the shack, for who could resist sneaking a look when you knew there was no-one at home?

As Jimmy put his head in the door there was a roar and a burst of flame and with a shriek Jimmy fled, his wet shoes slipping and slopping, back to the stream. The heavy footsteps of the caretaker firedog, the biggest firedog of all, were close behind him. Jimmy ran as fast as he could, with the animal's fiery breath on his back and sparks and the smell of fire flying past him. But he didn't catch alight! In all the confusion and fear of the moment he suddenly knew why! He was dripping wet! Jimmy was wet all over with wonderful water, first from the storm and then by his splashing in the stream. Every bit of him was soaked. No firedog could ignite him. So that was why they ran from the storm! He was saved— well, as good as saved. Back in the bubbling water, Jimmy turned breathlessly, and with sudden courage, to face his foe.

The huge firedog was puffing and blowing fire and bellowing and leaping about angrily on the bank.

He was trying to reach Jimmy with fiery breath but the water below prevented him. Each time he puffed fire and smoke, Jimmy splashed about more and the flames died. The firedog was very angry but he also looked extremely foolish, making all that fuss and effort for nothing. Safely wet, Jimmy decided that this was the moment to speak.

'Now look here,' he started in a small voice. Before he could gather himself sufficiently to know what he was going to say next, to his great surprise, the big hairy creature suddenly stopped stamping about. He appeared to be listening! Jimmy, gaining confidence at this favourable reaction, cleared his throat and spoke again, this time a little louder.

'Just what do you think you're doing?'

The firedog grunted and shuffled from one foot to the other. He looked embarrassed and unsure. He'd never been spoken to like that before.

Jimmy took a slow deep breath, and summoned up more courage.

'You're, you're just a bully. A big coward. And I think you firedogs are very mean to roam around here terrorising the forest creatures. I won't stand for it.'

Jimmy was shaking inwardly but he remained calm and looked the firedog directly in the eye.

Unbelievably the ferocious firedog appeared to be shrinking in size. No longer did he tower over Jimmy. He seemed to be growing smaller, and smaller and smaller under Jimmy's gaze.

Feeling astonished and very powerful, Jimmy opened

his mouth to continue his reprimand. As he did so the fire-dog shrank a bit more. Jimmy saw with amazement that he was actually shrinking this fierce creature with his words. The ferocious firedog was now just the size of a kitten and looked almost as cute as he began to prance and puff little breaths of fire no greater than a tiny spark.

'I'd better stop shrinking you before you disappear altogether,' Jimmy said.

Jimmy climbed out of the water, for there was no way that the little creature could harm him now. Jimmy bent down and gently picked him up, holding him in the palm of his hand and marvelling at what had happened.

'You look much better this size,' said Jimmy. And then he wondered, 'Tell me, is it magic that shrank you? If it is, how long will it last — and when are you likely to return to your big bossy size?'

The firedog was looking rather sulky, but not at all fierce any more. He scowled and shook his head in confusion.

'Well, I don't know what that means,' said Jimmy boldly 'but it serves you right anyway. Perhaps you'll explain it later when you get to know me. In the meantime look at this mess! You firedogs are destroying this magnificent forest. You're untidy and dirty and you obviously don't look after anything. And you've made all the birds and animals afraid, and they do nothing to hurt anyone.

'You firedogs are a pack of vandals and you deserve to be punished. How do you ever expect anyone to like you if you spend your time being selfish and mean and destructive?'

Jimmy had never spoken so much before in his life, and

52

his explosion of words was causing more shrinkage. He stopped speaking, realising what was happening.

'Oh, I see. You only shrink when someone is standing up to you? Not when I'm being pleasant to you?'

The tiny firedog nodded sadly.

He was now looking guilty and to Jimmy's surprise, instead of trying to breathe fire or be cross, he put his head down in shame. His big eyes looked sad and the little fellow was now so small that Jimmy began to feel a bit sorry for him. He patted him gently on his tiny head and said kindly, 'Well, you do see what I mean?'

The firedog nodded sadly again and for the first time spoke in a squeaky little voice.

'No-one has ever told us we were bad. No-one has taken any interest in us at all. We didn't know that trees and things were important. Where we come from there are no trees left. It's all black and fiery. I suppose we've destroyed it all,' he added woefully. 'So we come here to amuse ourselves. We hide from humans, and we thought birds and animals were there to be eaten. We like rubbish because we're not used to anything else and we don't know how to look after things. And because we have nothing to do and we're bored, we wreck things. That makes us feel important.'

The little firedog paused and scratched his ear. 'I suppose we really want someone to help us, that's all,' he said, 'and now that you've found us it's too late because I've shrunk. The others won't be my friends either because I'm not tough any more.' And he gave a long sigh.

By now Jimmy was really feeling sorry for the little

creature but seeing the waste all around jolted him back to reality.

'Well,' he said very gently so that the firedog would stay the same size, 'I'm sorry you're lonely and bored. I understand what that feels like, too, you know. But I'm learning now that you don't make friends or become happy by only doing the same thing all the time.

'You firedogs have to be stopped for the sake of the forest, but you also have to be stopped for your *own* sakes, because you'll only become more and more miserable if you continue to live as you have been living.'

The little firedog was so ashamed that he covered his face with his tiny paws and tried to hide inside his mane.

Jimmy put him down on the ground, and the little firedog started to walk back to the shack but being so small he hardly made any progress at all. He did a great deal of slipping and sliding while trying to climb through the burned sticks and rubbish on the way.

'Race you there,' Jimmy teased, but then he reproached himself. 'Come on,' he said kindly. 'I'll carry you.'

Now the firedog started whimpering and Jimmy realised that it was *his* turn to be afraid. 'What's the matter?' he asked.

'If the others find me like this they'll hate me. They'll board the spaceship and return to Uptight without me. I'll never fend for myself because I'm so small, and anyway I don't know how to do anything but wreck and destroy.' With one big gasp he concluded, 'And I can't even make enough fire to cook my dinner.'

'What if they don't find you?' asked Jimmy.

54

'They will. They'll search, because I'm the caretaker. I'm supposed to be minding the camp.'

'Mmmm,' murmured Jimmy, 'you *do* have a problem.' All of a sudden Jimmy had an idea. Carrying the little fire-dog carefully, he left the dismal site of destruction.

Chapter 9

As Jimmy strode along there was a spring in his step that had never been there before. Adventure had certainly come his way. The world wasn't such a boring place after all! He wondered how it was that these exciting things were happening here in the country and he knew that Mrs Fender had something to do with it, even though all she had done was to show him how to relax and sit still. Jimmy's thoughts took him back to how good it had felt being still. Somehow he was feeling different too — and the question he had asked himself once before came to him again: was stillness *really* the magic that was opening up his world? Jimmy thought about this a lot as he carried the shrunken little firedog into the greenery of the forest where Miranda lived.

A watery sun now provided warmth after the storm, and Jimmy's clothes were starting to dry. The track was not very wet so Jimmy set the miserable little creature down, speaking gently.

'Be very quiet and look around. What do you see? Look closely.'

The firedog turned his big, sad eyes on the scenery. Soon from among the grass a small finch appeared. At first it was barely visible, because its soft brown feathers blended so closely with the earth. It was searching for worms as they made their first appearance after the rain.

Jimmy pointed to an army of ants following their leader, a bee balancing on a flower, three ladybirds in search of a home, and lizards disguising themselves in the crevices of a rock. Everywhere the firedog looked he saw gentle things wanting to live peacefully, and for the first time in his miserable life he knew a flicker of happiness. Now the firedog, too, was having a new experience.

'This is our wonderful world,' said Jimmy proudly, knowing that he was only just learning to appreciate it himself. 'You and I have a great deal in common,' he confided. 'I used to get bored and frustrated and I used to bluster and push my way around, too — not in the same way as you did, but it brought the same results. I was missing out on the best things, just as you have been.'

'Now,' he went on, 'there is someone special you must meet. Someone who is responsible for your present state, really,' he added.

The little firedog was panting to keep up and kept tripping over pebbles, so Jimmy put him in his pocket and set off towards Miranda's nest.

When they were almost there, Jimmy said quietly, "Listen, you little firedog, I want to introduce you to Miranda. She's a beautiful white bird, a duck to be exact, whom you firedogs terrified. I have to show her what you are really like, and that there's nothing to worry about. But I don't know your name.'

There was silence.

'Well?' asked Jimmy.

'What's a name?' squeaked the firedog in a muffled voice from Jimmy's pocket.

'It's what you are called,' said Jimmy. 'Now, I'm Jimmy. Who are you?'

'I'm a firedog,' said the firedog.

'I know *that*. But don't you have your own special name?'

'Not that I know of,' the voice in the pocket replied.

'Well, I'll give you one,' said Jimmy. He thought for a moment. 'How about Chester? I have an uncle Chester.'

The firedog's face appeared from Jimmy's pocket, grinning from ear to ear.

'Your name is Chester. Now we'll tell Miranda,' Jimmy said, calling her name. 'Miranda! Miranda, come out. It's quite safe. I want you to meet someone.'

After a quiet quack or two Miranda appeared, ruffling her feathers, her eyes curious.

'Whom do you wish me to meet?' she asked in her most ladylike manner.

'Miranda, this is Chester,' said Jimmy. 'Chester, this is Miranda.'

He pulled the tiny firedog from his pocket and put him down beside the duck. She was almost six times his size!

Miranda looked the little creature over from head to toe. Then she looked at Jimmy. '*What* is this?' she demanded.

'This is Chester, the caretaker firedog,' Jimmy said.

'But, but…' quacked Miranda in amazement. It was unlike Miranda to find herself lost for words, which amused Jimmy. He threw himself down on the grass and told her everything that had happened since he left. The poor little firedog stood silently, looking very ashamed of himself. When

59

Jimmy had finished his story Miranda asked, 'But where are the rest of these creatures? Are they all shrunken? And what are you going to do with this one?'

Miranda was not instantly drawn to this ball of fur, and she wanted everything tidied up.

'No, they're not shrunken yet, but they soon will be. I'll see to that. This little one can stay here with you, can't he?'

Miranda didn't look too pleased.

'Oh, come on, Miranda,' pleaded Jimmy. 'The others will be mean to him if they find him like this. If you don't mind him, no-one else will. He's too small to hurt you now and he's far too small to look after himself.'

Miranda nudged the firedog with her bill, testing his mood. The creature moved closer to Jimmy.

'See,' he said. 'Chester is scared of *you* now. Won't you please set a good example and keep him warm and safe until tomorrow?'

'Oh, very well,' said Miranda reluctantly. She knew she had to help Jimmy and take care of the firedog. Jimmy placed him in Miranda's nest.

'Now, don't speak crossly to him,' Jimmy said. 'We don't want him to disappear altogether!'

Jimmy watched Miranda waddle towards her nest. She settled into her bed of grass and folded a protective wing over the little alien. Then, giving Jimmy a wink, she tucked her head down and closed her eyes.

Darkness had begun to fall. How fast this day had gone!

Jimmy yawned and stretched. He was tired. He sat down on a flat grey stone and leaned back against the trunk of a large gum tree. He closed his eyes. Although his muscles ached and felt really tense, he remembered not to hold them tight but to let the tension flow away. The aching gently faded and ceased. Jimmy's racing thoughts gradually quietened, and the stone beneath him no longer felt hard. A few minutes later when he opened his eyes, Jimmy was surprised at how refreshed he was. Being still for a while left him feeling almost as though he had just wakened from a restful sleep.

There was no sound of the band of firedogs. Jimmy decided he would worry about *them* tomorrow. He had seen enough adventure for one day. And though he didn't know it then, as Jimmy walked in the direction of Mrs Fender's house, in his heart the tiniest of true smiles was born.

Chapter 10

Mrs Fender glanced at the clock on the wall and observed that six o'clock had just passed. Moments later she heard the click of the front gate and the sound of Jimmy's footsteps.

He was ready for a hot bath, food and a soft pillow. But his face was glowing and Mrs Fender knew that his day had been successful.

This time Jimmy didn't tell her about all that had happened. A little mystified, Jimmy felt he should pinch himself to make sure he was not living in a dream. The whole day's activities seemed improbable. Yet in the bath, as the hot water cleaned away the mud of the forest, he knew that something very different from anything he had ever known was happening to him. He could hardly wait for the sun to rise again. He had so much to do tomorrow.

When the sun did rise, Jimmy dressed quickly, ate his breakfast and helped clean up. He said, 'I shall probably be out all day. Is that okay?'

'Yes, you have my permission. You seem to know your way about the place and you'll be quite safe. Are you enjoying your stay here now?' Mrs Fender asked with interest.

'Oh, yes. Yes I am, Mrs Fender. I'm really glad I came. But…' Jimmy hesitated.

'Go on.'

'Well, about my smile. Everything else is good. My head doesn't ache and my throat isn't sore any more, but I don't seem to have found a smile anywhere. I mean, I'm having a great time, and I don't even want my computer, or miss the TV. But what about the smile?'

'It takes time, Jimmy. Don't be in a hurry. It will appear when it's ready to, and when it does you will know. You won't even need to ask me,' Mrs Fender assured him.

'Smiling has something to do with sitting still like you showed me, hasn't it? Is that magic?'

Mrs Fender laughed softly.

'If you mean abracadabra and that sort of thing,' she said, 'the answer is no. But sometimes a kind of magic can be found in very simple, natural things. That's real magic because it makes things happen.'

'Well, things *are* happening, Mrs Fender.'

'That's wonderful news, Jimmy. I'm sure your smile will turn up very soon.'

Jimmy's eyes shone with expectation at her words. How eager he was to get on with his search!

'Well, I'll be off now,' he said.

'Very well, but whatever you do, don't forget to practise your stillness first. That's *very* important.'

Jimmy was hurrying out the door and he pretended he didn't hear what she said. There was no time for sitting around. He had lots to do and he felt far too happy to need to sit still and waste time. Anyway, yesterday he had done so at least three times. He could do without it today. He was on his way as fast as possible to Miranda's nest, and adventure.

Miranda was up and about, quacking and pecking but looking slightly annoyed. She looked relieved to see Jimmy. 'This creature you've left me to mind says it's hungry, but all I have is snails and leaves. It wants a barbecue! Or baked beans on toast! Or hard-boiled eggs! Eggs indeed! If it wants food, *you* have to feed it.' She waddled away to continue her own meal.

Jimmy was fascinated by this outburst from the duck. However, he had nothing to barbecue and no hard-boiled eggs. Chester was sitting dejectedly on a rocky ledge and looked so miserable that Jimmy knew he must try at least to find him something to eat.

The little firedog squeaked, 'In our shack … there's food there. Oh, I would love a sausage, or even a bone to gnaw on …'

'OK,' said Jimmy. 'I'll go to the shack. I just hope your big friends haven't returned. I've not been able to work out how to tame them yet.'

Jimmy hadn't gone very far when he had a funny feeling that he was being watched. He stopped and looked around. Everything seemed normal: blue sky, shady trees, delicate ferns swaying a little, a thick carpet of leaves, and quietness, except for the forest sounds and the ripple of the water nearby. Jimmy moved on. A twig cracked under his foot, startling him. Further upstream a rabbit darted across his path and Jimmy's heart jumped. He paused again, still feeling as if someone was watching or following him. He crossly told himself that he was imagining things and marched on. But the feeling persisted. When two magpies swooped from the heavens to drink at the stream, Jimmy swung around in terror, his eyes wide and his heart thumping wildly.

'Why am I so scared today?' he asked himself, biting his lower lip. He supposed that it was because he was going to the firedogs' camp. He walked on, more timidly than before, wishing he had not promised to get the tiny firedog some breakfast.

Jimmy was coming to the burned part of the forest now, closer and closer to the shack. He had the strong desire to turn and run away. But the face of the hungry little firedog was clear in his mind. He couldn't disappoint him now. He entered the clearing. The shack was quiet, and there was no sign of anyone at home.

Shaking and trembling, Jimmy made his way to the entrance. He went inside. The room was dark and damp and smelled of fire. It was very untidy and Jimmy had to be careful not to trip over things scattered on the floor. In one corner stood an old cupboard. Jimmy wished his heart would not make such a noise and wondered if his legs would continue to hold him up — they felt very wobbly right now.

He crept towards the cupboard and opened the door. It was completely empty. A rickety table standing nearby was bare as well. Over the fireplace hung a large pot. Jimmy peeped in. It too was empty. As a last resort, he looked behind the door. On the floor there was a basket. He lifted the lid, and there he found tins and packets of food — real camping stuff. Imagine firedogs eating ordinary food! Then

Jimmy noticed the writing on the tins was back-to-front, the same as the wrappers he'd seen littered on the beach. His heart did a flip as he remembered that these creatures belonged to another planet. This food had not come from an ordinary old supermarket but from somewhere up there in space. Snatching up the basket in haste, Jimmy dashed out the door. Only when he was away from the shack and out of the clearing would he feel less afraid. He ran across the clearing and down to the path by the stream. He ran on and on until he scrambled in behind some bushes to catch his breath, the basket still clutched tightly in his grasp. He thought he might hide there for a while. It seemed safe.

There was nothing to fear here. But Jimmy's breath was short and he was still shaking. The handle of the basket was cutting into his fingers, because he held it too tightly. And his shoulders and neck and face ached a lot. Jimmy Candlestick was strung tight again, like a spring about to break. The sun had gone behind a cloud and the forest seemed gloomy now. Jimmy felt uneasy. Where was yesterday? And happiness? And fun? And adventure? He felt tired and lazy. He couldn't be bothered any more. He would take the food to the little firedog and go home, back to Mrs Fender's and sleep. Then he'd listen to some music or watch TV or … but oh, no, Mrs Fender didn't have a radio or a TV! Jimmy felt defeated. He hadn't even remembered to bring an apple. Nothing was good today. Nothing.

Jimmy shivered. Now he was cold too. Well at least he would be warm if he went back to the house. Slowly Jimmy rose, still clutching the basket, and stumbled back to the path.

He had almost reached Miranda and Chester when he turned a corner and there in his path, glaring at him and breathing clouds of fire, stood two huge, ferocious firedogs.

What happened next was a blur to Jimmy. Quick as lightning, the creatures picked him up.

'Caught you, you thief,' they boomed, seeing the cans falling from the stolen basket. 'Intruder, rascal, villain, toad,' they snarled and chorused.

Jimmy struggled to be free, kicking and screaming but the firedogs were three times his size and Jimmy had completely lost both his courage and his composure.

He found himself being carried away, not back to the firedogs' shack, but downstream towards the sea.

The empty basket still hung over his arm.

Chapter 11

The firedogs strode on, dragging Jimmy and breathing fire. They were nearing Miranda's nest now and Jimmy, searching the landscape with terrified eyes, hoped that Miranda and Chester were safely out of sight where he had left them. As well as being very frightened, Jimmy felt angry — angry with Miranda for involving him in the first place, angry with the tiny hungry firedog for being hungry and, most of all, angry with himself. Today had gone very badly and suddenly he knew why. If he had only sat *still* for a while this morning, his mind would have been clear, he would have acted more carefully, and not rushed ahead without thinking. He would have been calm. He might have reasoned with the firedogs there and then, maybe even shrunk them with his words. Now he was a prisoner — captive, afraid, and useless. At these thoughts, two large tears sprang to Jimmy's eyes and rolled slowly down his cheeks.

Meanwhile, Miranda had observed what was happening to Jimmy. Although she herself feared the firedogs, she had no intention of allowing them to run away with her new friend, and without hesitation she scooped the miniature firedog under her wing. Swimming and flying, she crossed the stream as the unhappy trio passed by. Jimmy's eyes were too blinded by tears and the firedogs were too noisy and surrounded by too much smoke to notice a plump white duck and a shrunken little firedog dive into the basket and pull the lid shut as it swung from Jimmy's arm.

As they neared the shore the firedogs became loud and jolly, so pleased were they to be bringing Jimmy to the chief firedog. Jimmy trembled in their grasp as he saw the great silver space ship ahead. The door gaped open, ready to swallow him up and ferry him to some distant planet, to be lost forever. He struggled feebly and then gave up as the hairy paws of the firedogs tightened their grip, pushing him on, up the steps and into the craft.

The space ship seemed bigger inside, much bigger than Jimmy expected. The maze of corridors, rooms and doorways confronting him were like nothing Jimmy had ever seen on television. Space-age machines and hardware were everywhere. Flashing lights and computer screens were working continuously. For the first moment in his life, Jimmy hated the sight of keyboards. Certainly the entire ship was controlled by machines. Huge robot vacuum cleaners moved about, picking up and tidying everything that the firedogs had dropped and littered as they lumbered about. Jimmy, crammed between his two captors, could see now why the firedogs were so careless and untidy in the forest. The prisoner was carried all over the ship — in this door and out again, up those stairs and then down, back and forth, round and round until he was quite dizzy. The firedogs were searching for their chief. At last he was discovered, hiding under a table, munching his way through packets and packets of space-style raspberry marshmallows.

He was an enormous firedog, nearly as large as Chester had been before Jimmy shrank him, and he certainly was very greedy and selfish, for he was quietly gobbling down all the marshmallows by himself.

Jimmy was disgusted but still quite scared.

'Look at what we've brought you,' his captors bragged. 'A thief, stealing our food from the shack.' They grinned, and leered at Jimmy.

At the mention of food, the chief poked the last of the marshmallows into his mouth and climbed from his hiding place with a hopeful expression on his face. Jimmy was flung towards him, while the basket (and its secret contents) went flying in the opposite direction. The chief still had his mouth full.

The two captor firedogs pushed Jimmy closer. 'Surely you're pleased with us. This is the first human we've ever caught. Humans are supposed to be intelligent and useful. He can be our slave.'

By now the chief had swallowed his marshmallows and was peering closely at Jimmy, who was still scared and help-less, but furious, too. To be captured by such creatures was a terrible indignity. He began to feel like protesting, but it was of no use. He was locked in a space ship and surrounded by huge, hairy, ferocious firedogs. He waited to hear what his fate would be.

The firedog chief, however, had eaten too much. Con-sequently he was far too sleepy to be bothered thinking. 'Tie him up,' he grunted, trying to sound as if he knew what he was doing. 'We have no need for slaves, but he might be useful to us when we get to Uptight. Yes, he just might, especially if he's such a good thief. Tie him up.' And, with that, drowsily the chief ambled off to find a corner in which to have a snooze. So Jimmy found himself being dragged away once more, and no-one noticed that the lid of the basket, tossed into the corner, moved ever so slightly as its occupants peeped from within. Miranda and Chester were watching to see which way Jimmy was taken.

The two captor firedogs threw Jimmy into one of the cabins, after pushing and pulling him down a narrow passage. The room was dimly lit and was hot and stuffy. With strong, thick rope the firedogs tied Jimmy to a chair, slammed the door shut and disappeared. Jimmy was alone and lost in a dark and mysterious place. Presently there was an exploding sound as the space ship's motors crashed into action. Jimmy's heart leapt in his throat and his tummy turned over several times.

Jimmy's thoughts were running wild, 'This is so scary, being tied up in this suffocating little room, all alone without any possibility of escape. There is no one to help, no one even to speak to. Worse still, no one knows where I am or why I'm a prisoner. I'll be lost forever. The firedogs will probably roast me for dinner and no-one will know. If only, oh, if only none of this had happened.'

The more Jimmy worried, the more miserable and afraid he felt and more tears began to trickle from his eyes until he was quietly sobbing and the tears were salty on his tongue and his shirt was all wet.

While Jimmy was busily crying and feeling sorry for himself, the space ship was busy, too. The roar of the engines had quietened a little, settling to an even throb, and between his tears Jimmy saw the shoreline fall away as the craft rose on its legs and marched, rumbling and lurching, into the water. Further and further out to sea they waded, rounding the headland that Jimmy had not yet even explored. For a moment the engines seemed to stop completely as the ship lowered itself on its legs, poised like a giant spider about to pounce on its prey. Then with a whoosh it dived into a great dark underground tunnel, down into the depths of the sea. The ship pressed on, plunging into a churning tangle of water and air and darkness, foaming and frothing and tossing, and the world became dark. Over they turned and around they went, swirling further towards the end of the universe. Alone in this experience, Jimmy was very, very frightened.

In another part of the ship, Miranda was also afraid, but Miranda had Chester with her for company and she knew just what was happening, as Chester's tiny voice supplied a commentary.

'First we have to go through Darkness Cave, which is a natural rock formation, and the strong current helps to speed us along. No ordinary ships could go near it or they would be wrecked or swallowed up by the sea.

'Very nice to know,' quacked Miranda, mockingly.

'Well,' said Chester, slightly annoyed. 'At least you're safe on this craft. This is an uncrashable craft, I hope you realise.'

However, Miranda was thinking of Chester's large friends and could only ruffle her feathers and murmur, 'Small comfort. What happens next?'

'Next is the Passage of Time. That's a long corridor down

73

through Earth, which we firedogs discovered. We're the only space creatures to use it — it's *ours*. Sometimes we stop on the way to look for gems or precious metals.'

'Thieves,' snapped Miranda.

The little firedog ignored her, hoping her scolding word wouldn't shrink him further, and went on. 'Then we fly out at the other end of Earth. This is the best part.' He became excited at this and his tiny bounces of enthusiasm caused the basket to rock and roll all over the place.

'Settle down,' cautioned Miranda. 'You'll draw attention to us here, and I'm not ready to be devoured by your furry friends just yet.'

'Sorry,' said Chester, 'but this is really good. The engines roar and roar and we zoom into the atmosphere, way, way up in space on our way to Uptight.' His face fell then and he stopped speaking.

'And?' Miranda said, prodding him with her wing.

'Well, when we get there it's not so good. There's nothing to do except help ourselves to anything we want. And when we've taken everything we want there's nothing to do. So there's nothing to do at all to begin with, if you see what I mean, because we've already taken everything we want. It's boring. And this time, I'm so small that I daren't even show myself. If I did, I would be trodden on or something. Oh, everything is a mess, and I *still* haven't had any breakfast.' And Chester tried to roar and look fierce, an impossible feat.

'Well, I'm getting out of this basket,' quacked the practical Miranda. 'It's far too squashy in here. Anyway now that I'm in space and about to be caught and roasted the least I can do is to have a look around first, *and* find Jimmy.

You're coming, too. We've got to set him free.' She nudged the side of the basket so that it tipped right over. Miranda and the shrunken firedog climbed out.

'Come on. They went this way,' said Miranda, stretching her beautiful wings.

'Oh help,' grumbled Chester. 'If the others catch me like this I'm in big trouble.' Thereupon he tripped over an abandoned marshmallow, bumped into the leg of a chair, and added, 'If those vacuum cleaner things see me I'll be swallowed up like a piece of rubbish.'

Miranda, feeling hungry, gobbled up half the marshmallow (wishing it were a snail) and gave the other half to Chester as she swept him under her wing once more, waddling as softly as she could off down the passage where Jimmy had disappeared.

They were lucky. There were no ferocious firedogs in sight.

Chapter 12

In all the time that the ship whirled through Darkness Cave, Jimmy was not only tied to the chair but apparently glued to it as well. He had ceased his sobbing and now sat hunched, with every muscle tight, staring at the blank wall in front of him. He had no wish to look further, for the swishing and murky blackness made him feel sick and reinforced his fear. Waves of clamminess and chattering teeth overtook him. Never had poor Jimmy Candlestick felt so scared. Then in the middle of his misery Jimmy remembered the storm on the beach — his first real storm. Was *this*, everything that was happening now, any different from a storm on the beach? The storm was scary at first, but he had weathered it, hadn't he? In all the rain and the wind and hail and thunder and lightning, hadn't he *let go* and allowed his fear to leave him, in the way Mrs Fender had taught him? Could that work now, to calm the storm within him? Surely not. Nothing so simple could help Jimmy out of this dreadful situation — could it?

Suddenly Jimmy came to a realisation: no one but Jimmy was responsible for his present jam. Therefore, no one but he could get him out of it. He must do something to help himself. Taking a massive breath, and letting it out slowly, Jimmy closed his eyes. This was not easy to do, as he believed he needed all his wits about him but still he kept them closed, remembering Mrs Fender's sunny verandah and how good it had felt to sit there, still and quiet. She had told him to let everything go, and not to try, or concentrate on *anything*. So now, in all this turmoil, Jimmy did just that, and, little by little, first his body and then his mind began to calm down.

The mysterious depths of planet Earth were rushing by outside, yet Jimmy could have been back on the warm sunny verandah with the fragrance of flowers in the air. As each new wave of fear tossed and buffeted him, Jimmy let it go. He did not fight his fears. His muscles, aching with tension, began to relax. Next, his teeth stopped chattering. Slowly and gradually, the trembling eased until it stopped. His breath, which had been rising and falling like an earthquake, quietened and the pounding and fluttering of his heart slowed too. Ever so gently Jimmy felt his fear subside. No longer was he overwhelmed and sick with fright; the stillness that had surrounded him before returned to clear his mind and renew his strength. Jimmy remained still. After a time, he roused himself slowly from this peacefulness and opened his eyes. He was calm and brave again, and his previous terror became excitement. Here was a challenge Jimmy had not met before, and to his surprise his plight now made him feel happy.

'I can do it,' he thought. 'Somehow I'll get out of here and I won't be ordered around by those firedogs. I won't let anyone down, not Miranda, Chester, Mrs Fender, nor Dr Smiley. Most of all, I won't let myself down. And Jimmy

Candlestick *smiled*. A triumphant spontaneous happy and *true* smile beamed from him and came from the depths of his heart. The more he smiled, the happier he became. Dr Smiley was quite right when he had said that smiling was the most important part of getting well again, whether you've got the measles or you're just plain scared. Jimmy's joy was immense and his smile turned to silent laughter, for he had become responsible for himself, without robots or computers to help him in any way at all. So there, from the stillness, was the kind of magic Jimmy had been waiting for!

Just at that moment Jimmy heard a whirring, flapping kind of noise.

Suddenly the door burst open and to Jimmy's amazement and delight, in flew his loyal friend Miranda, with Chester on her back. The little firedog tumbled straight onto the floor, completing three somersaults before he found his balance. Miranda rose on her yellow feet and with outstretched wings quacked her relief and pleasure at finding Jimmy, safe and sound, and *smiling*.

Then Jimmy and Miranda both began to laugh. True, happy laughter! In order to get through the door Chester had balanced on Miranda's back in mid-flight, spun around in circles to twist the door knob open and finally somersaulted onto the floor. Now he staggered around, dizzily trying to work out just where he was. Finally, Chester looked up to see Jimmy's bright and kindly eyes smiling down at him.

'Sorry to laugh at your expense, Chester, but you did look funny. You're really cute when you're small. Thank you. Thank you both so much for coming to my rescue.'

Jimmy wished he could pick the two of them up but of course he couldn't as his hands were firmly tied. So his smile of gratitude grew broader and broader until it touched Chester's heart and for the first time in *his* life, Chester the caretaker firedog smiled completely, too! As he smiled, Chester began to grow. Suddenly he was the size of a kitten again. This made him so happy that he smiled and grinned more and more and consequently he grew faster and faster until he was restored once again to his original size.

Jimmy and Miranda could hardly believe their eyes. Chester's size and strength were restored, and all because *he* had found reason to be happy, too. So Jimmy's happiness was spreading to make others happy, and in a truly magical way, lots of things were improving.

Chester quickly untied Jimmy and the three friends hugged each other and laughed and danced and quacked around the room.

'Oh, this is great!' Jimmy exclaimed. 'Everything is going to be all right for everyone. Now, tell me. However did you both get here?' Miranda and Chester told him their story.

Jimmy was very impressed, especially by their courage, and he assured them that they were the best friends a boy could ever have. Moments later there was a roar as the ship's engines changed speed and the three felt a great lurch upwards.

'That was our take-off for space,' said Chester in a big deep voice, jumping up and down.

Miranda looked worried.

'It was bad enough in the basket when you were the

size of a mouse. We'll all go through the floor if you bounce up and down like that.'

Chester smiled at her and stopped bouncing, and the three of them felt the ship leave Earth.

Chapter 13

As they travelled through space, Jimmy, Miranda and Chester stayed hidden in the room in which Jimmy had been imprisoned. Now that he had found his smile and his friends, the room no longer seemed dark and stuffy. Even the sky through the window shone, scattered with stars of gold, but none looked better than planet Earth, now fading into the distance.

Jimmy thought of his home in the city and of all the things his family owned. Compared with never ending space, it all amounted to nothing. Even Earth itself looked very small. He pictured the freeways and all the traffic and saw nothing like that among the stars.

As they journeyed on, Chester explained that the space ship belonged to the planet Uptight and was programmed to travel between there and Earth. Jimmy wanted to know more about where they were going, but Chester said, 'Wait until we get there. Then you will see for yourself.'

'Well, what are the firedogs taking me there for?' persisted Jimmy. 'Surely I would have been more useful to them on Earth?'

Chester thought for a moment.

'I think they only wanted to scare you at first. But they

also wanted to steal you, because stealing is the only way they know how to live. 'I'm not going to steal any more,' Chester added, pleased with himself.

'I'll make sure you never have to,' said Jimmy.

'And when *will* they go back to Earth?' interrupted Miranda nervously, looking for somewhere to hide. 'I'm afraid I shall be part of this evening's dinner.'

'I won't let them touch you,' said Chester. 'After all, I'm the biggest firedog even if I'm not the boss. We'll be landing soon, so we should make a plan for your safety. Yours too, Jimmy,' he added.

However, there was no time. Noisy voices bellowed in the corridor outside.

Jimmy drew a deep breath to prepare himself calmly, and stood firm. The door burst open and there were the other firedogs, all pushing and squashing each other, each trying to get through the door first. The firedog chief won the battle, and the others followed. They were stunned. Jimmy was no longer bound to the chair but was standing before them with a delicious duck in his arms, flanked by their caretaker dog.

The chief leapt forward greedily to snatch Miranda. Jimmy flung Miranda in Chester's direction and turned, face to face with the chief.

'How dare you!' shouted Jimmy, raising clenched fists. The chief blew fire and smoke.

'Stop that at once,' Jimmy demanded in reply, choking slightly but not giving up.

The other firedogs drew closer, sneering and breathing fire, believing that Jimmy was cornered.

Chester was just about to intervene when Jimmy launched into his biggest speech, giving the firedogs a piece of his mind in no uncertain terms. Dozens of strong and brave words and phrases sprang from Jimmy's lips. He pointed out their selfishness, their cowardice and their cruelty.

The five ferocious firedogs shrank and shrank, and all their fire and smoke disappeared.

Five miniature firedogs grizzled and grumbled and stumbled about, completely confused at this turn of events.

'We need that basket again,' Jimmy cried.

Chester fetched it and soon all the firedogs on board were comfortably packed into it.

'Now for Uptight, Jimmy. When you have seen all you want to, we can get back to Earth again,' the big firedog Chester said.

The little firedogs protested squeakily in vain.

There was a grinding sound as the space craft slowed down and a few minutes later the adventurers were waiting to disembark.

Chapter 14

'Oh look,' cried Chester as the space ship shuddered to a halt. 'We've come in on the bright side of the planet. We've never done that before. We usually land on the dark side. I suppose that's because you're with us, Jimmy. This is where all the goodies are. Usually we creep in on the dark side and then have to sneak along to the bright side at night when no one is looking.'

'What's the difference?' asked Jimmy.

'The dark side is where we firedogs belong. I'm afraid it looks rather like the burnt-out forest where we camp on Earth.'

'Oh no!' exclaimed Jimmy. 'You firedogs really know how to wreck things.'

Chester looked ashamed once more, but his new-found happiness made shrinkage impossible and he disapprovingly glanced at the basketful of squealing firedogs.

Miranda, who wanted to get going, fluttered her wings. 'I'm starving,' she quacked. 'At least if we've landed on the bright side I can hope for a light luncheon of snails and insects. Now I have something to look forward to. Come along everyone.' In her fussy, organising manner, she led the small procession down the steps of the space ship.

Brilliant sunshine greeted them. Not surprisingly, the bright side of Uptight was a glittering and colourful place. Where the ship landed was no ordinary airport. It wasn't even like the space centres shown on TV. From the landing pad stretched vivid green lawns divided by brightly paved paths widening into highways leading in many directions. Large, neatly-spaced trees stood tall, bearing the biggest, reddest fruit that Jimmy had ever seen.

The visitors moved closer, following the paths that lead to this wonderland. Everywhere he looked Jimmy observed a richness and splendour that was more impressive than he had ever seen, anywhere, before. Uptight was magnificent, and not at all as Jimmy expected, having known the firedogs and their way of life. Everything was shining and everything was beautiful. Yet Jimmy was puzzled. There was something strange and eerie here. He stood quietly, taking it all in.

Not a cloud was in the sky, and not a puff of wind blew the leaves on the trees. There was no sound but their own footsteps, and there were no voices to be heard, or bird songs in the trees. Not a speck of dust littered the paths, for the breeze was not there to blow it. This was no gentle stillness but a mysterious emptiness.

Chester broke the silence.

'Let's go sightseeing,' he cried. After all, we're here as tourists now. I've never seen the place in the daylight before. You'll be really interested, Jimmy, and Miranda, too, of course,' he added hastily as she drew herself up in indignation.

'Well I *am* curious,' she said.

The three of them were moving closer to the buildings in the distance.

No other figures could be seen anywhere. The place was lifeless. Miranda's bright black eyes were searching the grass for her lunch, and the basketful of firedogs had ceased their squealing and were now chatting together amiably in tiny voices. As the group moved further from the space craft they saw lawns more frequently dotted with fruit trees. Miranda darted under them seeking a snack among the fallen leaves, but there were no fallen leaves! Miranda, looking mystified, tilted her head questioningly. Jimmy and Chester were moving on so she waddled as fast as she could to the next tree, where more scuffling and more disappointment followed. Miranda was becoming cross. There was no lunch, and she was being left behind as well. She began to quack, quietly at first and then in crescendo.

'Jimmy Candlestick,' Miranda rose to her feet, spread her wings and flapped wildly.

Jimmy spun around and stopped in his tracks.

'Miranda, what's wrong?'

'There are no snails. No earthworms. No insects. No *leaves* even!'

'Oh Miranda,' Jimmy sounded exasperated. After all, he was hungry too, and poor old Chester must by now be ravenous.

'Try another tree,' he said. 'Look, over there, the one covered in huge apples.'

'Oh, yes. Right, I'm on my way.'

She scuttled across, and Jimmy and Chester followed.

Plonk. A giant apple dropped at Jimmy's feet and rolled away. Jimmy looked about for more, hoping for one like Mrs Fender's.

Just as Miranda had said, there were no fallen leaves to be seen.

'Amazing,' murmured Jimmy.

Miranda shook herself crossly.

'There are always grubs around fruit trees,' she declared. 'There's something odd here. Where is that big apple, anyway?'

They all looked around for the huge crimson fruit, but it had vanished. Above their heads, more giant fruit hung suspended, glowing red like balls of fire.

'They're not apples!' exclaimed Jimmy. 'Look, they're strawberries! I've never seen anything like them. Look at the size. Why, you could feed ten people from just one of those strawberries. And what are strawberries doing up on a tree, anyway? Wow!'

Just then another strawberry fell, missing Miranda by a hair's breadth. It, too, rolled quietly away and the group watched as it settled on a conveyor belt on the lawn and was instantly transported silently towards the city.

'Look at that,' shrieked Jimmy. 'Automatic harvesting!'

Chester shrugged.

'Well, that's what it's like here. Let's move on.'

Miranda shook herself again in irritation and reluctantly followed as Jimmy ran to investigate the rest of the trees. The next one bore pears, suspended like grand lanterns of gold. Beside it, a thick vine climbed skywards and from it flourished masses of purple grapes, each single grape the size of an orange. When they found the orange trees they saw branches bowed by orange basketballs bobbing and swinging in abundance.

Some of the trees and vines were still in blossom. Great flowers in pink and white clusters trailed low on the ground and the air hung thick with their heavy perfume.

The adventurers were drawing closer to the buildings now, and the green expanse became splendid gardens, dense with exotic foliage in full bloom and decorated with sculptures and magnificent works of art.

There was no sound or movement except for Miranda's pecking and scuffling in her persistent search for food, but the flowers, in all their glory, held no tender morsels for her.

'I'll pick you one,' Jimmy suggested, hoping to cheer her up.

He ran to a twisted bush laden with red roses, three times as big as any he had ever seen. Jimmy selected a perfect bloom and snapped his nail clippers over its stem. The stem would not break. Jimmy tugged a little, then he pulled and struggled with all his might but the rose remained firmly upon the bush.

'I can't do it. Chester, you try.'

Chester tried too, but he couldn't remove the rose.

'They must be unpickable,' Chester grunted.

'And look,' said Jimmy excitedly. 'It's a rose, but there are no thorns. There are no prickles at all! They should have prickles, even I know that.'

'I don't know much about them,' said Chester. 'We fire-dogs are not interested in flowers — only food, really.'

As he spoke, several flowers began to fall, first from the rose bush and then from surrounding trees. Like the strawberries, they too slid onto the conveyor belt and before Jimmy's eyes, assembled into a magnificent bouquet, wrapped and tied as a gift. The bouquet moved past them, off to the city.

'I must be dreaming,' said Jimmy. 'Look, the fruit is massive and automatically harvested. The flowers are unpickable. There are no leaves or lawn clippings on the ground, and there is no food for Miranda. There's no breeze or any sign of life at all. Not a sound. And look at the sky. It's clear blue. There's not a cloud to be seen. I'll bet it never even rains! Look at those fountains. The water is there right enough, but it doesn't flow. Why, there's nothing natural here at all. Come on. I want to see the rest. You'll have to wait for food, Miranda. Here, I'll carry you.

The tourists moved towards the city.

As they drew nearer, Uptight burst into life. Traffic suddenly began to arrive on the roads as if somewhere, by someone, a time switch had been thrown. First, several cars appeared, travelling so fast that they almost flew. Then a glistening train whooshed by, its windows dotted with staring, expressionless faces, which was the first sign of people on the planet. Along came several buses. Chester hastened them all into one of them saying, 'Let's see the rest in comfort.'

No other passengers were aboard and the bus had no driver.

'It's automatic, too!' Jimmy exclaimed.

'Oh, yes,' Chester agreed. 'We're on a conveyor belt, the same as the fruit and the flowers. Look outside.'

'Heavens, so we are.' Jimmy said excitedly, peering out of the window. 'All the cars and trucks and buses are following the same route, round and round. Here comes the train again, too. This is the strangest place.'

'Well, we *are* on another planet don't forget,' put in Miranda.

'Yes, but no one seems to have any choice as to what they do or where they go,' observed Jimmy.

'What do you mean, no one? I *see* no one. No one at all,' the duck replied. 'Only faces at a train window. Who lives here anyway? I always believed Uptight was inhabited by firedogs, but there must be other inhabitants. No firedog would live in this neat luxury, would they Chester? I want to find out!'

Chapter 15

As Miranda spoke, the bus entered an area where houses like palaces stood among manicured lawns, perfumed rose gardens and splendid statuary. Here the travellers observed more activity.

Figures appeared, taking up positions like actors upon a stage. They all seemed to have a task assigned to them. Artists stood with brushes. Golfers swung their clubs. Footballers and cricketers jogged dispassionately but as if in training. Others pretended to wield their racquets or bounce balls of various shapes and sizes. Some were ready for a swim. Further afield were dancers and musicians, apparently rehearsing, while next to them horse riders prepared to race. No one was working. All were occupied, but aimless.

'There *are* people, Miranda,' said Jimmy.

'Yes, but they seem weird,' she quacked.

Now the shopping mall came into view and the bus took Jimmy and his friends past the stores. Vast riches and luxuries were displayed, and in the food stores banquet tables presented their offerings, laden as if for a feast. Uptight was certainly a land of plenty. Although there was nothing wanting, everything seemed very strange. The people, so well dressed and poised in this or that position, were waiting, woodenly aimless. Their only movements were uptight, rhythmic and monotonous, like life-size puppets.

Sounds were growing louder. Engines throbbed, voices were heard and loud music rang out as the million noises of a city came alive. Here were the jangly bangly noises of the city near Jimmy's home but on Uptight they were even louder, yet the place remained *lifeless*. The people's faces, though painted bright and beautiful, were expressionless, like the empty portrait of Jimmy that Mrs Fender had drawn. There were certainly no true smiles from deeply within!

Jimmy stared in amazement. The planet Uptight somehow reminded him of his life back home. The magnificence of the place mirrored all the inventions Jimmy had always enjoyed but, really, there was nothing enjoyable about this at all.

Jimmy thought longingly of the countryside near Mrs Fender's house, the forest where Miranda lived, and the splendour of the sea. Uptight had none of those things. Uptight was absurd. It was artificial and without feeling.

The bus was travelling away from the city now and returning to where the space ship had landed. It seemed that the visitors had been shown everything and the time had come to leave. Jimmy was pleased to be going, though he was still lost in thought, considering everything he had seen. Miranda, too, was quiet, having abandoned her search for food, and Chester was content to hold the basket of firedogs, waiting patiently for Jimmy to decide what they should do next.

Finally Jimmy spoke.

'It's dead,' he said flatly. 'The whole planet's dead. Those people, the fruit, the flowers — they are all imitations. There's not a bird or an animal in sight. There are no fallen petals or spider webs. There's not even a garbage bin. There's not even any garbage. Everything is perfect, but it's not perfect! You can't have perfection without *im*perfection. What's the good of huge ripe red strawberries all the time? Or perfectly scrumptious chocolates? What's the good of perfect sunshine and blue sky and not a drop of rain? What ever made Uptight like this?'

The basketful of firedogs began to babble all at once so Chester spoke on their behalf, and Jimmy and Miranda listened intently.

'A very long time ago the planet Uptight was a satellite planet of Earth. The very clever people there invented and constructed anything and everything to make life absolutely perfect — and fantastic. Any single thing you wanted was possible at the flick of a switch. Unfortunately, no one really had anything left to do but enjoy it all.'

Chester went on.

'The satellite planet was so perfect, so automated and mechanised, that life became artificial, and terribly boring. Although it was boring, the inhabitants were living under great pressure and at a tremendously high speed. The planet spun and spun and spun into a tight ball which broke away from Earth's atmosphere and drifted into the solar system, becoming the planet Uptight.'

'We firedogs were family pets on the satellite planet. When the planet broke away from Earth, everything the people needed was obtained by mechanisation. In fact, the whole place is run by machines. The people became like robots, so they didn't need pets any more. We just wandered away to the dark side of the planet. We dogs were friends so we stuck together. We were pretty sad and lonely but we began to fend for ourselves over there. I suppose we just learned to grow selfish and greedy and ill-mannered in order to survive. Instead of being happy and smiling and wagging our tails, we became angry. We turned into sort of monsters and we learned to breathe fire and scare others. As you have discovered, Jimmy, we had no one to discipline us. We took what we wanted in every way.'

Chester paused for breath.

'After we'd lived like that for quite a long time, our group found out about this space ship and the opportunity to re-turn to Earth and help ourselves to more. You see, the natural environment that animals need has just about disappeared on Uptight and all the other creatures are gradually becom-ing extinct. It was important for us to do our best to survive.'

Chester spoke thoughtfully.

'I have a lot to thank you for, Jimmy. You've helped me to change. I know now what it means to *care*, and I too can smile and be happy.'

Jimmy squeezed Chester's paw and said, 'It's interesting how much creatures can learn from each other, isn't it? Es-pecially when we help one another.' He gave Chester one of his wonderful new smiles and a hug, and Chester smiled back and they laughed together with the sheer joy of being alive. Miranda quacked cheerfully, her wise head tipped to one side.

'Come on, Miranda,' said Jimmy, sweeping her up into his arms, ready to go. 'I'm getting off this bus. I'm getting out of this place. It gives me the creeps. If this is the bright side, I'm glad we're not going to see the dark side. Now that I understand the story of Uptight and how it all happened, I'm going to make sure you firedogs don't have to come back here, either.'

The little firedogs began to chatter rapidly again, and Chester said, 'They're asking for all those goodies they were coming here to get, to take back to Earth.'

'They don't give up easily do they,' laughed Jimmy speaking loudly above the noise and clamour in the background. 'OK, we'll let you loose then. Help yourselves.'

The bus had stopped and Jimmy, Chester and Miranda jumped off, tipping the basket over until the five small firedogs fell out. Their confusion was incredible. They couldn't walk fast enough to make any progress anywhere. They slid on the conveyor belts and were bowled over by cakes, chocolates and cherries in transport. And they were in constant peril from all the traffic zooming past. A few minutes was more than enough. Five shrunken firedogs were scared and instead of stealing and plundering the forlorn little creatures could only scuttle and hide and scramble for their lives.

When he felt they had learned a good lesson Jimmy gathered them back into the basket. Calmly and kindly he explained that all their old ways were now out of the question.

'Planet Earth is the best place for you to remain,' he said, 'as long as you behave.'

They all nodded enthusiastically. Then Jimmy told them that when they arrived back on Earth, he would find them a good home near the forest where they would be looked after and live as normal lovable dogs again.

Immediately, the little firedogs understood and began to show appreciation. One by one, their tails began to wag, their ears to prick up and, finally, they were smiling. Very soon the basket was bursting at the sides as the five little firedogs gradually returned to their original size.

Without further ado, everyone went back to the space ship, leaving the planet Uptight to continue its miserable existence.

When they were aboard and the ship's engines roared into life, Jimmy went to the control room. What a wonderful opportunity to have a go at being a real astronaut!

Chapter 16

It was a happy group, indeed, that travelled back to Earth. The firedogs were certainly no longer ferocious and were quickly being transformed into the friendly furry pets they had been long ago. They now regarded Jimmy Candlestick as a hero for the part he had played in restoring their lives. They had even learned to be friends with Miranda. Jimmy felt very pleased and proud. He knew that without each and every one of them he would never have found the contentment that made him so happy now. Most of all, he knew that he would never have gone in search of contentment without the skill and the strength of quiet magic to help him on his way.

Now from the control room of the space ship he was glad to be returning to his own world. The voyage was not scary this time. Instead, Jimmy was able to enjoy the approach to Earth from this great height. The ship re-entered the Earth's atmosphere and continued its descent until the once-distant mountains now seemed close enough to touch. Jimmy gazed in wonder at the scene and imagined he was in charge of the whole world, speeding home to rescue it from the fate of Uptight.

'I will, I will, I will,' he said over and over to himself.

'Never will I let the world become as fast and blank and dead as the planet Uptight.' He stroked Miranda's feathers just to feel again their silky touch, knowing that in this one gentle bird there was more real perfection than in all the gadgets ever invented.

In no time at all they had emerged from Darkness Cave and were moving through the waves towards the beach.

Jimmy picked up Miranda, and the group left the ship. It was good to be home.

The dogs bounded on ahead and then returned to Jimmy and Miranda, bouncing, barking and yapping, for they had no need to use words now that they were real dogs again. When Jimmy seemed to take no notice of their request, the biggest one, Chester, tugged at his sleeve and whined a little, pulling Jimmy in the direction of their old shack in the forest.

'Okay, I'm on my way,' Jimmy cried. He and Miranda, puffing and quacking, followed the bouncy dogs until they came to the firedogs' part of the forest.

The six lively animals now sat with their ears pricked and tongues lolling, glowing with proud and happy expressions. Their eyes were telling Jimmy to *look*! Jimmy looked, and to his surprise the burned forest did not appear to be nearly as bad as he had remembered it. Certainly it was still burned and trampled. But, wonder of wonders, among the blackness of the branches about him, Jimmy could see tender green shoots — the first of the new life to come.

Everything was all right. The forest would survive after all, and order had been restored. Just then the sun smiled through the branches, casting a soft light upon the scene,

102

and Jimmy heard rustling and twittering close by. Miranda quacked and leapt from Jimmy's arms to dive with her bill among the blackened leaves, just beating a flurry of wrens to the first worm to return since the fires. She looked very pleased with herself, much to the wrens' disappointment, but it made Jimmy happy that Miranda should be the one to discover that nature was in harmony once more.

'Well, come on, all of you. This will grow without us watching it. I have to find Mrs Fender. She probably thinks I'm lost.'

He gathered up the ever-hungry Miranda once more and, with the friendly dogs following, ran up the rise and over the bridge to the road towards Mrs Fender's house.

They found her in the garden, working with her sketchpad and she gave Jimmy and his companions a warm and wonderful welcome. Mrs Fender was very pleased to see them. Chester was the first to introduce himself by gleefully fetching a stick, placing it at her feet and waiting for an approving pat, first for himself and then for his friends.

Mrs Fender obliged.

'And this is Miranda?' she then asked, stroking the lovely bird's head.

'It sure is,' Jimmy began. But he didn't know how to continue. Perhaps there was no need to explain anything. It was so complicated. Maybe everything, all those wonderful adventures, had been just a dream? Didn't his story seem too unusual to be real? But of course it was real! He was holding sweet Miranda in his arms and surrounding Mrs Fender were six of the friendliest, bounciest, most appealing dogs you could ever find. And there on his finger was a healing wound.

103

It was all real. But he couldn't explain. He could only smile and smile and smile.

Mrs Fender needed no explanation, no words. She already knew the secret of quiet magic and anyway, Jimmy's eyes told the whole story.

Holding Miranda gently, Jimmy began his good-byes.

'I wish I could take you all home, but I can't,' he said. 'In any case, you'll be happier here near the forest, with open space and each other for company. Stay friends now, won't you, and thank you, Miranda, for helping me grow up.'

Jimmy handed the lovely bird to Mrs Fender and she snuggled into her arms. Quacking quiet words of approval, Miranda gave Jimmy a long last look and one of those bright and beautiful eyes winked knowingly, as if to say, 'Aren't we clever?'

Jimmy's sadness at their parting was soon dissolved by the dogs who sat before him with the big question in their eyes, 'Where are *we* going to live?'

He fondled each one in turn and when he came to Chester, Jimmy said, 'I'm going to ask Mrs Fender to find a special home for you all. I know she will, won't you Mrs Fender?'

'Of course,' she said. 'I have just the very place for you. But first, I think you'd like some dinner?' At the mention of the word the dogs enthusiastically sprang to their feet.

Jimmy grabbed Chester and held him tight for a long moment. 'Be good,' he said, 'and be very, very happy.'

Chester bounced a lot and licked Jimmy and they both laughed together.

'Thanks a million, Chester, I really love you!' cried

Jimmy, and he gave Chester a final pat as he bounded off with the rest of the dogs following Mrs Fender towards her kitchen.

Jimmy stood silently, alone. This moment reminded him a little of when he had first arrived here. He was alone then, too, but what a different boy! So much had happened in such a short time. How long had it really been? Perhaps a day or two, or was it a month, or even a year? It was all so magical, one couldn't be sure. He'd journeyed the heights and depths of the universe in that time. He'd made discoveries that *were* a kind of magic, and he'd come to understand so much. He had found his smile! Jimmy was now ready to look in the mirror. He began to walk slowly towards Mrs Fender's studio and saw her coming to meet him. She was carrying his bag, some apples and something else as well, his portrait.

Jimmy was excited but a little shy, too. He took the portrait from Mrs Fender and looked at it hard and long. It was complete. To see himself in paint now was just like looking in a mirror, but a new one. Before him was a face with shining eyes, and a very happy smile. The face Jimmy saw now showed exactly the way he felt within. And Mrs Fender had even included a few freckles!

'From being in the sun,' she explained, with a knowing look.

Jimmy rubbed his nose thoughtfully.

He beamed up at Mrs Fender, pleased with the finished product.

'My smile arrived most unexpectedly,' he said. 'Finding it wasn't all good fun, either. But now I've got it, and having it is worth everything that ever happened to me. Thank you for showing me how to begin.'

Mrs Fender took Jimmy's hand and pressed it warmly.

'I congratulate you, Jimmy. It takes courage to start a journey such as you've made and you've succeeded in every way. Your search is over. Now, may I hang your portrait with the others?' she asked. 'It's a good likeness and I will enjoy having it there on the wall.'

'Oh, yes, please do,' said Jimmy, 'It will help you to remember me, too.'

'I'll always remember you,' Mrs Fender assured him. 'Now, young man, the plane is on its way. It's time to say goodbye.'

Jimmy felt torn between sadness and joy, and for just a moment a lump rose in his throat.

Mrs Fender, guessing his thoughts, calmly went on.

'You've lots and lots to look forward to, you know. This first adventure will always be the most special, but now there's nothing to stop you as each new adventure comes your way. Enjoy them all, Jimmy.'

'I will,' said Jimmy. He was quiet and confident as he spoke.

Then he added. 'Please look after Miranda and the dogs for me. I'll miss them a lot.'

'They'll be all right here, and *they'll* always remember you, Jimmy.'

Mrs Fender continued to hold Jimmy's hand and together they walked out of the garden and across to the track through the forest.

'I'll certainly never forget *you*,' said Jimmy thoughtfully. 'You knew all the time, didn't you?'

Jimmy flung his arms around Mrs Fender and maybe for the first time ever Jimmy Candlestick hugged another person. He really meant it, for he wanted to tell Mrs Fender that she was the wisest and, despite all her lines and crinkles, the most youthful person that he could have ever imagined. He tightened his hold on his bag, and with a wave and a smile all over his face, he ran down the track to the waiting aeroplane.

Mrs Fender waved, too, and stayed to watch him until he was out of sight.

Chapter 17

Within a very short time of boarding the aeroplane, Jimmy had watched the forest, the sea and the surrounding countryside fade into the horizon. Not long afterwards the aeroplane landed. No taxi was there to meet him so Jimmy began to walk home, as it wasn't very far at all.

His stride was easy and his heart was light, and he found himself humming a tune to the rhythm of his step. Everything was wonderful!

Today, here in the busy city, the sun peeped between the tall buildings, lighting the streets and bathing everything and everyone there in a glow of festivity. Perhaps the busy city was not so bad after all. Most of the people had friendly faces. They weren't plastic like those on Uptight. Here and there were patches of trees and flowers between the columns of stone and concrete. Jimmy had never noticed them before, and, although the traffic made a noise, Jimmy found that just occasionally he could detect the chime of a bell or the song of a bird, floating high above the city sounds. Was it possible, he wondered, looking about, that the world had *changed* while he had been away?

Soon he reached home, and he took the elevator up to the top floor of the building. His personal robot was waiting for him, with its lights flickering and alarms beeping, and all its joints creaking and groaning as it hustled Jimmy along the corridor.

Once more Jimmy was in the middle of the hisses, bangs, screeches, beeps and jangles of home, and he didn't like it one bit. All the mechanical things seemed to be out of control and at the same time the robot was pushing and urging Jimmy to hurry and unpack and sit down at the table. His dinner of chips and icecream was being served. As always everything here had to happen in a dreadful hurry!

Then and there, Jimmy stopped in his tracks.

'WAIT,' he shouted above all the commotion.

Without a moment's hesitation he reached for his robot's switch and flicked it *off*. The robot slowed down and froze. Then Jimmy ran to the robot at the table and switched it off also, and the icecream it held in mid-air began to trickle all over the place. Next, Jimmy ran around from room to room and up and down, flicking and switching everything off. The whole place became quiet. 'That's better,' he said to himself and he went into the kitchen. After pouring himself a long, cold glass of milk Jimmy returned to the living room and slid into the biggest armchair. As he drank his milk, Jimmy surveyed his home.

He saw comfortable furnishings in soft fabrics. He saw restful paintings and ornaments in shapes and shades that pleased the eye. Vases of fresh and fragrant flowers coloured the corners of the room. Silken drapes hung from the windows to filter the sunshine, and his feet were warm on the thick carpet. For the first time ever, in the evening light, Jimmy Candlestick *saw* the home he lived in. He saw it peacefully and quietly, without any distractions. And he suddenly knew that it wouldn't matter now if he became the poorest boy in the world with only a tent to live in. He could still find happiness because happiness was right there, within himself.

Finishing his drink, Jimmy placed the glass on a table and closing his eyes, he relaxed completely, and his body and mind drifted into stillness.

Here in his own home, Jimmy recaptured the calm and tranquillity he had first found on Mrs Fender's verandah, then in the shade of the forest, and later in the cabin of the space ship, tied to a chair. So he could find it *anywhere*! Now, as he sat still, far below in the busy city the rest of the world rushed on.

The minutes ticked by, and soon Mr and Mrs Candlestick returned home from work. To them the house seemed to be in chaos. Everything was quiet. Everything seemed to have stopped.

'There must be a power failure,' cried Mrs Candlestick. 'I'll check the spare generator,' shouted Mr Candlestick.

They both began dashing about all over the place in a great state until, not looking where the other was going, they collided right in front of Jimmy who had just opened his eyes and was stretching luxuriously.

'Good heavens! Jimmy! You're back already! What happened ... Are you better? ... Did Dr Smiley's prescription work?' Mr and Mrs Candlestick were speaking rapidly together.

Jimmy grinned.

'He looks surprisingly happy,' his father said.

'He's smiling. I've never seen him smiling,' his mother said, looking concerned.

'Why would he be sitting here smiling, when the whole house has broken down?'

'Mum and Dad … it's OK,' Jimmy announced, rising from the chair. 'The house has *not* broken down, and I'm smiling because I'm happy!'

His parents continued talking to each other at the same time, in anxious tones. Jimmy had never spoken to them like that before. Nor had they ever spoken very much to Jimmy. So now they didn't know what to say next.

Disregarding their concern, Jimmy went on.

'Come over here and sit down and I'll tell you all about why I'm happy.'

Jimmy linked his arm through his parents' and drew them to the dining table (which was now decorated in choco-late icecream).

Mr and Mrs Candlestick were greatly surprised to find themselves seated quietly, and listening attentively to Jimmy as he recounted his adventures.

He told them the whole story, right from the begin-ning. He told them about how lonely and sick and miserable he had been when Dr Smiley visited; he told them about meeting Mrs Fender and all he learned from her; he told them how his sore throat and headache almost magically disappeared; he told them about beautiful Miranda and how he had saved the forest from the firedogs. With spar-kling eyes he described the forest and the beach. Finally he told them the story of Uptight — the terrible tense and artificial planet. Then he explained that the firedogs, too, had learned to smile and so they were able to live happily ever after.

'Oh, I've learned so many things and had such a wonderful time, but the best lesson of all came at that moment in the cabin of the space ship. I was tied up and awfully scared and lonely, but when I realised that whatever happened to me next was entirely up to me, then things began to go right.

'You see, Mrs Fender had shown me the way to change and find strength through being still, but unless I put it into practice myself, its benefits would be wasted. No one else could do it for me, not Mrs Fender, not Miranda, not one or two or twenty robots, not even you two! Only I, Jimmy Candlestick, could help myself. So I did! I found the real Jimmy Candlestick! And when I could face my problem calmly, everything else just fell into place. I was able to make the hard things a lot easier — and so I'm happy!'

At first Mr and Mrs Candlestick were too stunned to utter a word, but gradually, in the silence of the room the frowns on their faces gently smoothed away. The three of them sat quietly looking from one to the other and back again, for some minutes. Then to Jimmy's amazement, Mr Candlestick's expression broke into something different from usual — a smile of understanding. Jimmy looked towards his mother and saw that she had happy tears in her eyes.

Something about his parents was changing too. Without all the background noise, the magic of stillness seemed to be entering the room in another way. Then Mr Candlestick began to laugh — a great big, happy, surprised laugh. He slapped the table with the palm of his hand and laughed even more as he gasped, 'Well, you wouldn't believe it!' over and over again.

Then Mrs Candlestick was laughing joyfully, too.

Jimmy felt a bit confused, for his parents had never behaved like this before.

Mr Candlestick bounded around the table to Jimmy, throwing his arms around his son.

'What a great boy,' he exclaimed, quite emotionally. Mrs Candlestick appeared at the other side of Jimmy and said, 'Isn't this wonderful. We had no idea that … that … we … um … ooh …' She was pink in the face and totally flustered.

Finally, both parents settled down and Mr Candlestick spoke calmly and gently and seriously.

'Jimmy, for all these years your mother and I have thought we were heaping happiness upon you. We've worked and saved and read all the right books. We've invested and bought and provided, just so that you'd be *happy*. But all the time what we were giving you was making you *un*happy'! Mr Candlestick paused reflectively. 'Do you realise that this is the first time we three have had a proper conversation?'

Jimmy nodded, and his mother hugged him again.

'Really, this family has been missing a great deal,' Jimmy's father went on. 'Jimmy, you've managed to grow up a lot without our help at all! You didn't need *things*! You needed directions. So did we all! If only we'd known.' Mr Candlestick shook his head and gave a long sigh.

'Oh my darling, don't reproach yourself', interjected Mrs Candlestick gently, 'nobody's perfect, least of all, parents. If it hadn't come to the stage where Jimmy *had* to go away and experience adventures in order to find happiness, he wouldn't have learned anything new. Nothing would have changed. We'd all just be going on the same as before. And I wouldn't be sitting here with my arm around him now, would I?' And she hugged Jimmy tenderly again.

'You're absolutely right, my love. Now we've all made a discovery. Jimmy, we've learned as much from you today as we've ever taught you.' Mr Candlestick paused reflectively.

'You know, it's not bad without all that noise and action around the place. I seem to be thinking more clearly. And it's nice sitting here like this together. It seems important to say, Jimmy, that we love you very much. How can we all remain happy like this?'

'I like the way things have changed,' Jimmy said thoughtfully, 'and all I want is for us three to stay friends always, because I love you both, too.'

His parents smiled and nodded and smiled some more. It was clear to Jimmy that his mum and dad were now feeling happier inside themselves, just as he was.

Jimmy took a deep breath. 'And I'd like to go to school and make friends with other boys and girls, and I'd like a dog like Chester.'

'Oh, yes, of course … that's easy,' his parents said at once. 'And with a pet and heaps of friends we'll all find lots of things to do together'. As they spoke a golden sunbeam streamed through the window, as if magically applauding their words.

'Between us, we have so much to enjoy — and so much to share. Let's begin straight away.'

And that's exactly what they did!

Afterword
DR ROB MOODIE
CEO VICHEALTH

Jimmy learns how to be still, to be at peace, and how to smile truly. By doing so, he discovers real joy, and the same time he learns how to cope with the sometimes difficult realities of his life. Jimmy learns how to trust others and how to share his smile.

We constantly yearn for happiness, but so often we look for it in the wrong place. We seek it in possessions, in others, in fame or fortune or influence, somewhere else. Jimmy is my hero, because he gets to know himself, and, in doing so, he *could still find happiness, because happiness was right there, inside himself* (p.111).

Share *Quiet Magic* with others. Read this delightful parable to your parents, read it to your children. Share it with your neighbours and friends, with your nieces, nephews and cousins.

May you be at peace and enjoy real happiness!

Dr Rob Moodie
March 2002